The Thames Murders

By Johanna M. Rieke

Paperback ISBN 978-1-78705-599-5
ePub ISBN 978-1-78705-600-8
PDF ISBN 978-1-78705-601-5

MX Publishing, 335 Princess Park Manor, Royal Drive,
London, N11 3GX
www.mxpublishing.com

Cover design by Brian Belanger
Translation by Bryan Stone

Dedicated to my dear sister, Lisa, who is always there when I need her

My practice

The interested reader will certainly recall the series of brutal murders in London in the course of 1890. They were a succession of gruesome killings, which were all committed close to the River Thames. By June there had already been five such deaths, yet, apart from the bestiality of the cause of death, there seemed no other connection between them. Scotland Yard had to admit the murders were still a mystery, and was severely under pressure from the more sensation-seeking newspapers. As a result of a barrage of scandalous reporting, many of their readers, already naturally alarmed, were in panic. For my part, although aware of these crimes, I maintained my distance, as I had now for almost a year had my own medical practice in Kensington.

During the adventure that came to be known as "The Sign of Four," I came to know Mary Morstan better, and as, at the end of the events concerning the Agar treasure, our hearts found their way to one another, I summoned up the courage to ask her hand in marriage. Her agreement made me the happiest man on God's earth, but the thought of having to leave my quarters in 221b Baker Street naturally weighed heavily upon me.

I well remember the day, as I searched for the appropriate words in which to explain my situation to my friend, Sherlock Holmes. It was late afternoon, as Holmes and I sat quietly smoking in our Baker Street rooms, in front of a roaring fire, with a cup of tea, reading *The Times*. Unexpectedly, Holmes suddenly turned to me and said, in a firm voice: "My dear Watson, I am quite of your opinion. The practice of the recently deceased Dr. Farquahar in Hornton Street will be ideal for you and your future wife, Miss Morstan." I looked at my friend in surprise, before asking: "Holmes, how did you know that I had yesterday proposed to Mary, and that she had accepted?"

"Come, Watson," replied Holmes calmly. "That was not difficult. I had already observed during our adventure of 'The Sign of Four' that you had felt very attracted to Miss Morstan. As you then one day brought her picture, in a silver frame, to stand on the small table by your armchair, I already suspected that our days together in Baker Street would one day come to an end. Three weeks ago, you asked me to pass you your cheque book, which had been here in our locked drawer. The next day there was, pressing out your waistcoat watch pocket, a small round object. I saw that you from time to time touched this object gently with your finger. At such moments, when I spoke to you, your thoughts appeared to be elsewhere. I had no doubt that you had purchased an engagement ring for Miss Morstan, and were carrying it with you while awaiting the right moment to propose. Yesterday evening, as you returned from the theatre, you were in in a most relaxed, almost joyous mood, and your pocket had resumed its usual outline. The explanation could only be that you had proposed to Miss Morstan, she had accepted, and the engagement ring is now on her finger."

I looked at him in amazement. "That is quite correct; it was exactly as you say. But how did you guess that I was interested in the practice in Hornton Street?"

"Not 'guessed', my friend, but 'deduced,' from the following sequence of facts:

1.   "You plan to marry.

2.   "You are a doctor, and will therefore intend to earn your living, for your wife and yourself, in your profession.

3.   "You were not recently in practice, and have therefore no established patients.

4.   "You have only limited financial resources, so it would be preferable to become a partner in an established practice, or, better still, to take over a practice becoming vacant.

5.   "During the last week, in the 'Properties' column of *The Times*, the practice and furnished apartment of the deceased Dr. Farquhar has been daily advertised.

As you see, Watson, taking these facts together, the conclusion was that you had found this offer of interest."

"You have again found your mark, Holmes. But that does not yet explain how you arrived at the conclusion that I had decided to purchase the practice. I had only reached that decision shortly before you spoke to me".

"That I had also observed, Watson," replied my friend. "For a week now, you have studied the property advertisements, and each day you had more intensely hung on the Farquahar notice. Today was just the same, but then you forgot your tea, as the full but cold cup beside you shows. Then your hand moved mechanically to your watch pocket, and you looked again at the picture of Miss Morstan. You took the cigarette, which you had only just lit, from your mouth, smiled, and then pressed out the cigarette most energetically in your ashtray. At that moment I knew that you had made your decision. You were, moreover, now ready to tell me about it." During this account Holmes had barely moved; he sat cross-legged in his armchair, and drew on his pipe, the eyes half closed. In admiration I had to say, "Wonderful, Holmes, you have described it all precisely." I had to add, a little ruefully, "I am truly sorry that I had not earlier taken you into my confidence." He smiled for a moment, and then opened his eyes, put down his pipe and stood up energetically. "Now, Watson, we will drink a toast to your new life. In anticipation of this moment, I had asked Mrs. Hudson to chill a bottle of champagne, and to have the glasses ready."

That was of course characteristic of Holmes. While I was weighing the right words to tell him what I had planned, he had already understood perfectly, and read my every gesture. Now, however, he insisted on reassuring me that I should embark wholeheartedly on my new life, with no fear that our already deep friendship might in any way suffer.

It was clear that I could no longer be involved in his cases, and learned of many of them only afterwards, when I visited him in Baker Street. These visits were, however, all too rare, as my growing practice demanded close attention. I often helped also in evenings, at weekends and in holiday times in St. Bartholomew's Hospital. The additional income was indeed a necessary help in repaying the purchase of the practice, which was the subject of a contract over some years.

My beloved Mary was a great help to me at this time, which was, at first, difficult. She not only managed the household, but also attended to the accounts and correspondence of the practice. But now was the start of the warmer season, in almost every doctor's surgery a quieter period. Mary and I would have more time for one another, and I could visit Holmes from time to time. It would not surprise me to discover that he had already solved the Thames murder mystery, and that I could again wonder at his lucid explanations.

A Visit from Lestrade

It was Tuesday, June 3rd, and I had made house visits to patients all morning. The afternoon had been occupied with appointments for patients visiting the practice. It had been a demanding day, and I was looking forward to a quiet evening with Mary. It was nearly five o'clock, and I was preparing my consulting room for the following morning, when there was a knock at the door from our apartment. The door opened discreetly, and Mary looked in. She asked quietly, "John, have you any more patients?"

"No, and there are surely no more today. Is there something wrong?" Mary never entered the practice without good reason. "Inspector Lestrade is here. He wants to speak to you. I fear he looks as if he is really at his wits' end."

Inspector Lestrade? Upon my soul, it seemed a long time since I had last seen him. What could have prompted him to visit me? I decided to receive him in the small study adjacent to my consulting room. A moment later I found myself face to face with this man who, in the past, had so often, with Holmes and myself, brought criminals to their just punishments. His features had not changed, being almost rat-like, with cunning eyes, but it did not need a doctor to see that this man was close to total exhaustion.

"Dr. Watson", he began at once without further introduction, "I would like to be discussing old times, but that is at this moment quite impossible. I come because of the Thames murders." He had a hunted look as he addressed me. I recalled, how he had in the past often arrived so impetuously in Baker Street, as if he were bringing the next storm with him.

"I am very sorry, Inspector, but I do not see how I can help you. What has Mr. Holmes told you?"

"That is a disaster in itself, because no-one seems to know where he is. Mrs. Hudson says he is somewhere in France, seeking to recover a painting stolen from the Louvre. In the Diogenes Club, I was able to speak to Mr. Mycroft Holmes, who disclaimed all knowledge of where his brother might be. He was most reserved, and I fear I was inclined to lose my patience, so that, although an inspector from Scotland Yard, I was escorted to the door."

Despite the earnest situation, I could not forebear to smile, for the Diogenes Club, with its complete ban on conversation within the club, save for the Stranger's Room, as it might disturb the quiet and personal privacy of its members, is certainly the most unusual club in London. "And so I came to you, Dr. Watson, in the hope that you might tell me, either, where Mr. Holmes might be found, or, perhaps, whether he has any ideas which might bear upon this terrible affair."

I had to disappoint him. "Much as I regret it, Inspector, I can give you no help at all. I last called on him in April, and at that time there had been no Thames murders. How long has Holmes been missing?"

"Mrs. Hudson said that he took a hansom cab five days ago, that is, on May 29th; he was going to Victoria station to take the Continental Express to Dover, and then the steamer to Calais. I have had enquiries made with the authorities at Dover and Calais, but they know nothing; there is no trace of Mr. Holmes. I therefore asked the Sureté and in the Louvre, and again, there was nothing. The Museum denied, indeed, that a painting was missing." "That might have been for tactical reasons, or even because of embarrassment," I interjected.

"Quite so, Dr. Watson, that also occurred to me, the more so since we never quite know with the French. With these foreigners one can never be quite certain. But I know some of the Sureté officers personally, and as I have confidence in their word, I cannot avoid a feeling that something is not as it appears to be."

A troubling feeling began also to take hold of me. Where was Holmes? Had he met with danger or misfortune on his way to Paris? Or was he in fact not there at all? But where then might he be? Lestrade suddenly spoke out aloud the thought, which obviously struck us both: "My goodness, Dr. Watson, Sherlock Holmes cannot leave London, cannot abandon London to its fate, while this city is overrun with this unprecedented murder series!"

We looked at one another without another word for a moment, before Inspector Lestrade took his hat, and turned toward the door. "I beg your forgiveness, Dr. Watson, if I have been a burden to you. I must return to the office where, who knows, perhaps there is more news. The expectations of public opinion, and of the new commissioner, are making severe demands upon me." He smiled briefly and added, "Please convey my respects to your wife."

With this, he took his leave, and disappeared, and I heard the house door close. I remained however for a few minutes, trying to put some order to the questions now tormenting me. I knew however that I would not find the answers here, in my consulting room. Tomorrow morning I would complete my round of visiting my patients, by making a call at 221b Baker Street, to see what could be done. Just as, a half an hour earlier, I had looked forward to my evening at home, I found that I was already eagerly anticipating the events of the next morning.

In Baker Street

The home visits to my patients the next morning were quickly dealt with. All of them seemed to be well on the way to recovery, so I could now concentrate my thoughts on my visit to Baker Street. I still had the key, as Holmes had insisted that I keep it. However, in view of the many alarming moments which Mrs. Hudson, our landlady, had experienced, both with us and because of us, I felt it more appropriate to knock at the door, to announce my visit.

I can hardly describe how pleased Mrs. Hudson was, to see me. She had made the tea, and we sat in her homely kitchen exchanging our stories. She asked about Mary, and about myself, and how the practice was developing. Then came my opportunity to ask, quite casually, about Holmes. She recounted precisely that which Inspector Lestrade had told me. She said that Lestrade had been there, and that he had been most troubled at not finding Mr. Holmes there, since Mr. Holmes had promised his help in solving the Thames murders. She had certainly found Mr. Holmes' departure curious, but she had already seen so many aspects of him, and of his sudden behaviour, that little could now surprise her. I could not begrudge her this attitude. Holmes was surely one of London's most unpredictable tenants, and yet I knew that Mrs. Hudson would not for anything consider losing him.

Apart from a truly affectionate and emotional farewell from this dear lady, and the confirmation of what I already knew, the conversation had delivered no indication of Holmes' mysterious disappearance. Perhaps I might, however, in our former rooms, find something useful. As I asked Mrs. Hudson whether I might go up and look around, she looked at me almost reproachfully, saying only, "It is not only Mr. Holmes who considers it important that you are always at home in Baker Street, Just go on up there now, and you will no longer disturb me in my housework," and with this, smiling, she began to clear the table and sent me out onto the stairs.

As I stood again in our former lounge, it seemed to me that time had stood still. As usual, Holmes' violin lay on the sofa, the Persian slipper with his tobacco lay in the coalscuttle, and the air was still charged with a smell of stale smoke and various chemicals. The floor was covered with papers, newspaper articles and notes. Another might have thought that a stranger had broken in and hunted for something particular. I, however, knew better. This chaotic condition resulted from Holmes' search for information. Mrs. Hudson and I knew this situation only too well. It was usually Mrs. Hudson who cleared up this disorder, but probably she had been instructed by Holmes to leave everything as I had now found it. That could perhaps mean that the scattered papers could help me to understand what was going on. I began therefore to pick up the papers and, at least, to put them in small, orderly piles on the table.

I had hardly completed this task, when I heard footsteps on the stair, coming quickly nearer. Suspicious, I called Mrs. Hudson, and ran to the door. Before I could reach it, it was violently thrown open, and there stood in the doorway the powerful figure of a man. I addressed him angrily. "Sir! What makes you think you can break in here like this? Who are you?"

The uncouth, and obviously inebriated, person took a step nearer to me. Instinctively I moved back, without taking my eyes off him. "Damn it, man, who are you and what do you want here?" I said as I sought to gain a moment to get nearer to the fireplace. This time there was an answer from my visitor, who was still advancing upon me.

"My name is Jack Potter, I'm a labourer in the docks, got that? This busybody Holmes has been going around the docks asking too many questions. What does he want to know about me?" As he spoke these last words, he shook his fist angrily, and his eyes flashed with an evil and malevolent rage. I felt the mantelpiece in my back, so I could retreat no further. "I can tell you nothing. Mr. Holmes is not here. Please come back at another time".

As I forced myself to speak these few words, I hoped that my voice was strong enough not to betray me. "If I can't catch up with that rat, Holmes, I'll have to make do with you, mate." As he said this, he lurched threateningly, two steps nearer towards me. I spun quickly round, grabbed the heavy iron poker, and turned back to face him, holding the poker protectively, like a dagger, before me. As I tensed for the attack, I heard quite unexpectedly a more than familiar voice: "My goodness, Watson, I fear this time I really went too far."

With these words, the mask fell away, and there stood before me a trusted figure. "Holmes!" I cried out in surprise, and let the poker slowly fall towards the floor.

"I regret deeply that I caused you such a shock, my old friend, but on the other hand, it shows me that my masquerade is convincing enough, if it even suffices to deceive such a close friend."

As he said this, his anxious expression gave way to a slight, fine smile. "Scotland Yard has a lot to learn concerning successful disguises. I think perhaps I should write a monograph on the subject. Let us first, however, have a glass of sherry. I think we both may need it."

A few moments later, we were sitting, smoking in our armchairs in front of the fireplace. I had in the meantime recovered from my immediate shock, but now I was somewhat annoyed. After all, I had let Holmes deceive me completely, and I was at the same time unable to share his pleasure at this childish dressing-up game, especially when Scotland Yard needed his help. And where had he been the whole time?

As I spoke to him, he became at once most serious, and explained, "Both my disguise, and my disappearance, were essential, if I wanted to make enquiries in the docks, without being discovered. This is a closed world, in which the guardians of the law can achieve little. An outsider who walks in asking questions will get nowhere. The dockworkers are like oysters; at the least sign of something new in their familiar surroundings, they close up and say nothing. One must become a part of them, in order to have any hope of seeing behind the façade."

"And did you find anything out?" I asked tensely. My annoyance had already given way to curiosity.

"At least some suspicions have been confirmed, but new ones have taken their place. The answers I have so far found to my questions have unfortunately only led to more questions, and the whole is like a ball of wool with a number of loose ends."

With these closing words Holmes seemed, sitting there, to be lost in his thoughts. His eyes were closed, and the fingertips of both hands were pressed together.

Suddenly he gave a start, opened his eyes, and launched into a conversation about my practice. I told him of the work, and from his gestures and reactions, it was clear that I told him nothing new. That could not now surprise me, for I knew how he could read the inner thoughts of a person as if he had an open book before him.

It was already drawing on to evening, and Mrs. Hudson appeared, to suggest an appetising evening meal. I felt myself torn, for I was tempted to stay, but must naturally think of Mary, who would surely be awaiting my return and beginning to wonder what had become of me. Again, as if he had read my thought, Holmes spoke: "Please don't be anxious, Watson. As I returned I had already asked Mrs. Hudson to send a message to your wife, that you were visiting me and would be home later."

Surprised, but reassured, I took my place at the table, now thoughtfully prepared by Mrs. Hudson. After dinner we sat smoking together, and spent some time on reminiscences of our past cases. I did not venture to ask about the present dilemma of the Thames murders, as I suspected, after his rather vague remarks of the afternoon, that he was not yet ready to talk about it. It was already a little after eleven that I took my leave of Holmes. I was no sooner on the stairs, than I heard the melancholy sound of his violin. I then knew that Holmes, now alone, was searching for a solution to the Thames murders.

As I arrived home shortly before midnight, I was surprised to see light in the study. I opened the door to find Mary at the writing desk, her arms folded on the table and her head resting on them. I looked at her for a moment as she slept, and then ran my finger gently over her cheek. She first blinked and looked up without understanding, and then sat up and said sleepily: "John, are you back already?"

"Already is not quite the word, dear, it's nearly midnight."

"Oh," she murmured, and smiled quietly. Then, although she was obviously very tired, she asked me how Holmes was. I described very quickly my experiences and impressions. She thought for a moment and then said: "The Thames murders are obviously a very serious problem. I think Holmes needs you." I looked at her in surprise.

"What do you mean?" I asked.

She replied clearly: "Whenever Holmes has had a particularly difficult case, you have been his faithful friend and companion. He would surely value your help now, but he will not ask you directly."

"And why not" I asked suddenly, interrupting her.

"Because he will not ask you to give up our already limited free time to be with him, when he knows you would wish to be with me."

There was silence for a few moments, but before I could reply, Mary continued, "John, I treasure every free minute that we can enjoy together, and I had hoped this summer we could be alone together, but I cannot allow that you do not give Holmes the help he obviously needs." She smiled at me, threw her arms around me and kissed me and then continued: "I therefore expect that you go to him tomorrow and tell him that it will be just as it was, when we met one another; you will be at his side."

"Your word is my command, my dear", I replied cheerfully, as I took her by the arms, swung her round me and led her up to the bedroom. "Tomorrow I am at Holmes' side, but tonight I belong here with you."

Return to Baker Street

After breakfast, I first asked my neighbour, Dr. Smythe, who had his own practice, whether he might, in the next three weeks, be able to look after my patients. I had often helped him, my younger colleague, from time to time, and so it was reassuring that he was very pleased to be able to offer some compensation. The first problem was therefore satisfactorily resolved.

In the meantime, Mary had written to reply to an outstanding invitation from Mrs. Cecil Forrester, with whom she had earlier found employment as a companion. For Mrs. Forrester, Mary had been practically a daughter and confidante. The two had also remained in contact after our marriage, which so far had been limited to written correspondence. Mrs. Forrester had already invited Mary to visit her in the country. Mary had now replied by telegram, and during the afternoon there arrived a messenger with the reply, which was as follows:

Dearest Mary,

I would be delighted to receive your visit. I will be leaving in a week's time for Sussex, to spend the summer there, but in the meantime we can surely enjoy our time together in London, just as we did earlier. It would be a pleasure if you could come to my London apartment in Lower Camberwell today. Your husband is also welcome, but he has surely no time, as you have told me that he is now helping Mr. Holmes to hunt for the Thames murderer. May God preserve these brave men whose acquaintance it has been my privilege to make.

Please reassure your husband that you will be in my care during these days, so that he can concentrate on the problem now in hand.

Yours,

Cecil Forrester

Mary, as her feminine intuition had suggested, had already prepared for each of us the necessary baggage. As it was time for her to leave, I saw her into the waiting hansom, and she looked at me seriously. "Do promise, John, that you will take care, and not run any unnecessary risks."

"Be reassured, dear," I replied, kissed her and gave the driver his instructions.

Back in the house, I looked at my travelling bags and went quickly back to my study. Unlocking the drawer of my writing desk, I took out my old army revolver. I cleaned it and oiled it carefully, and dropped it into my travelling bag. It was time to go back to Baker Street.

As I entered again the familiar rooms, I was enveloped in a dense cloud of tobacco smoke. The air could have been cut with a knife. Although I also enjoy smoking, I had to find a window on the other side of the room, and, I succeeded, in opening it and allowing fresh air to enter. Opening a second window, the air helped to lift the dense fog in our living room even more rapidly. Now, however, I could see Holmes' gaunt figure, sitting on the sofa with knees drawn up, dressed in a nightshirt and dressing gown, with his long arms round his knees. His hair stood up wildly, and on his usually clean chin the stubble of his beard was already apparent. He looked almost like a sick cat, which had no longer cleaned itself and appeared uncared for and abandoned.

Holmes had closed his eyes, and one might think he were sleeping, were it not for the regular drawing on his pipe. This pipe, which I knew well, was appropriate to the situation. It was a most unappetising object, in which the leftover remainders of yesterday's tobacco were collected, dried, and then smoked again. Should the reader ever find himself confronted with the smoke of such a pipe, my advice, as a doctor, can only be, to move away from it quickly!

This, however, I could not do. The sight of my old friend, in such a desolate state, went to my heart. I had in my ears the words of Mrs. Hudson, as I arrived, that Mr. Holmes had spent the whole night playing unmusically and tunelessly on the violin. That he had today eaten nothing, only added to my concern. As his old friend I might have spoken differently, but this time the doctor in me spoke up: "Holmes, for goodness' sake, you cannot treat your body in this way. No food, no sleep, and too much tobacco will be the end of you."

Slowly, as if awakening from a deep sleep, Holmes opened his eyes. "Watson, what are you doing here?" His stare fell upon my travelling bag on the floor. "You are not planning to go away, and so to take leave of me? Or even worse, is there a difference between you and your wife, after I made such demands on her yesterday?" His expression showed real anxiety.

I replied firmly, "No, my friend, it is none of these things. I have come to stay with you, just as long as it takes to solve the Thames murders. That is, of course, only if you need me and would like to have me at your side."

Just as the flame of a candle, when almost extinguished, burns suddenly more brightly with new wax, so sudden was the change which went through Holmes. The lassitude, even resignation, fell away. He jumped up, took a step towards me and set his fine, but strong, hands on my shoulders. During the questions that followed, which he directed at me, his eyes never left my face. "You are truly ready to accompany and support me in clearing up this affair of the Thames murders?"

"Yes, I am."

"And what about your practice and your patients?"

"In the summer the practice is quiet, and in an emergency, my neighbour, Dr. Smythe, will represent me. So, as you see, Holmes, I can indeed spare the time."

"And what does your wife think of this?"

"It was she who urged me to come to you."

I saw the doubtful expression on his face give way to a warm enthusiasm. "But Watson, that is wonderful. I have truly missed you, but I would never have burdened you with my problems. But I must also congratulate you on your wife. She knows what is needed to make her husband happy, and is ready to give him the freedom to make it possible."

His words touched me deeply, and as I did not know what to say, I only nodded silently. "Before we start to involve ourselves in the case, Watson, we should build up our strength. What do you say to a good dinner at Simpson's?"

"Why, gladly, Holmes," I replied, delighted at the energy and vigour which he now radiated.

"Very well, then, and I will attend to myself. In the meantime, you may make yourself welcome in your old bedroom". With these words he disappeared quickly into his room, and as I unpacked, I heard him busy with his wardrobe.

My bag was quickly emptied, and as I turned, saw Holmes ready in the doorway, freshly shaved and combed, waiting with his silk hat and overcoat, as he said, "Come, Watson, old friend, come, and we will enjoy a superb dinner at Simpson's." He turned on his heel and trod lightly down the stairs. I let myself be caught by his enthusiasm, and followed as quickly as I could.

The Victims

The dinner at Simpson's was excellent. The conversation was mainly led by Holmes, who described to me a number of cases he had solved in the meantime, and also informed me of recent developments in the criminal underworld in London. It was only when we were back in our rooms, and had adopted our familiar places, that Holmes began to talk about the Thames murders.

"Now, Watson, what do you know about this affair?" he asked me.

"To be quite honest, only that which I have seen in the newspapers, and of that surely not everything," was my frank answer.

"Then it will be best if I begin by describing to you the various events from the start, in chronological order."

"May I make notes, Holmes?"

"Of course, Watson. Unless we have all the facts before us, we will scarcely find the thread that must run through all these crimes. Let me begin, then, with the first victim. His name was John Miller, 29 years old, married with four children, the youngest still a baby. He worked on the docks as a packer, and was said to be loyal and reliable. This was confirmed over several days by my investigations on the docks. On May 12th, early in the morning, around 4 o'clock, he was on his way home after a night at work. His body was found, two hours later, in Chilton Street. His pay was still in his purse, and his wedding ring was still on his finger. The next victim was Samuel Williams, 38 years old, an insurance clerk employed at Lloyds. He was also regarded as very solid and reliable. It seems that his only amusement was rat-baiting." Holmes paused for a moment, and interrupted his account. He blew the smoke from his pipe into an artistic ring.

"Rat-baiting? Really, Holmes, I thought that that dreadful amusement, of letting rats be chased and killed by dogs, and betting on the numbers killed, had long been forbidden by the law, under threat of heavy penalties," was my rather shocked reply.

"Of course you are right, Watson, but there are many clandestine places, such as empty warehouses, where these things are still done. But to return to the victim. On May 19th, Mr. Williams spent an uneventful day in his office, and then went for his evening entertainment to the vicinity of the Greenland Dock. It seems that he knew there was to be a rat-baiting match there. It is an insalubrious district, and he never arrived. He must have met his murderer beforehand in Rotherhithe Street, just before it meets Swing Bridge Road, near to the dock. Have you noted all that? Shall I go to the next victim?"

"I believe so, Holmes, but just a moment; how was it with his valuables?"

"Splendid, Watson, you are following carefully. Mr. Williams was still in possession of his gold pocket watch, his gold cufflinks, and a matching cravat-pin. And in his pocketbook was a considerable sum of money, with which perhaps he intended to place bets." While I completed my notes, Holmes poured us a whisky, sipped his glass and then carried on steadily with his account.

"The third victim was Miss Kitty, a person of about 21 years of age, but whom neither the police authorities nor I with my enquiries could better identify. We do not therefore know her real surname. I surely do not need to tell you what her profession had been. She was seen on May 24th, at around nine in the evening, in a public house called The Haven, which she left in the company of a man. Around an hour later her body was found, by customers leaving the establishment, in nearby Prince Street. No valuables were found, but I fear she may not have had any in her lifetime."

Holmes paused again, looked searchingly at me, and I asked him instinctively, "And who was the man with whom she was seen? If the police could find him, he can perhaps give some kind of information. Or might he even be the murderer?" My thoughts were racing, tumbling over one another, and the words came out without reflection.

Holmes looked at me calmly and said, with a faint smile, "The police have already found him".

"And?" I asked urgently.

"They found him, shortly after Miss Kitty's body was found, lying in the adjoining New King Street. He was the fourth Thames murder victim." I was shocked, and stared at Holmes as my simple train of thought fell in fragments around me. Holmes however carried on calmly with his description.

"His name was Nathaniel Cook, and he was fifty years old. He was a widower, and had been a soldier, until he was wounded and left the army as an invalid. In order to enhance his pension, he worked as a gardener in the Royal Park at Greenwich. His possessions when he was found were a golden pocket watch, a wedding ring, and his pocketbook. The fifth and last victim was Mrs. Sophia Walter, 43 years old, married, and with two almost adult children. She worked in Deptford Hospital as a nurse, and on May 28th her turn of duty ended at midday. She left to go home. When she failed to arrive at her usual time, her husband became concerned and went later to meet her. He found her body, not far from their lodgings on Bronze Street. She had been dead some time, and again, she still had her wedding ring and a small amount of cash in her purse".

As Holmes had finished his account, we both remained very quiet. Only after my whisky glass was empty did I feel ready to ask him again. "Holmes, you are quite correct; not one of the victims was robbed, and they were all found around the streets near the Surrey Docks, on the southern Thames bank opposite the Isle of Dogs; apart from that, they appear to have nothing in common."

With the help of my fingers, I went again through all the individual points, which I had noted. The victims were both men and women. They were both young and old. They had most varied occupations and were from widely varying social backgrounds. Even their family circumstances were different. The murders were irregular, and were committed at various times of day and night.

"My goodness, Holmes, it looks as if the murderer might be insane, and simply kills people at random. How can he be stopped?" Helplessly, I looked to Holmes and he weighed his next words very thoughtfully.

"Watson, you know my method, and you know that I can find no solution unless I have all the necessary information. At this moment we know too little and cannot justify any explanation." After a short pause, he stood up from his armchair, heavy with fatigue, and said, "Come, Watson, we would best now go to bed. At this moment, all we can do is wait."

Silently we looked at one another. I understood, all too well, that he expected there to be more victims before this mystery could be cleared up.

More Victims

On this night it was some time before I could find calm and sleep. Suddenly I felt a firm grip on my shoulder, and I heard from far away as it were, my name being called. Sleepily I opened my eyes, and there was Holmes, standing, already fully dressed, beside my bed. "Come, Watson, it's time," he said urgently.

"What time is it then?"

"It is already dawn".

My reaction, as I stared at Holmes, was not gracious, indeed one might call it severe, for I had hardly slept three hours. He explained at once: "Lestrade sent Constable Brown with a message. Mrs. Hudson was awoken twenty minutes ago and called me. Now I must call you".

As he spoke, I struggled to get out of bed and go to the washstand. With a splash of cold water in my face, I came back to life, and my head began to function clearly. As I dried myself, Holmes turned to leave my room. "What is it about then, Holmes?"

He turned around quickly, looked at me with bright eyes and said, "Didn't I tell you? There are two more Thames murder victims. Please hurry now, Watson, P.C. Brown has instructions from Inspector Lestrade to bring us directly to the scene of the crime".

Thanks to my military service, in an emergency I need only a short time to be dressed and ready. Ten minutes later we were in a police carriage, being driven towards Watergate Street in Deptford. During the journey, Holmes was very quiet, so I spoke briefly with P.C. Brown. The conversation was necessarily general, as he had not yet been at the scene, and did not know who the victims might be. As we arrived, there was already a small crowd, despite the early hour, who had to be held back, by the police, from pressing forward to the scene.

As we alighted from the carriage, Inspector Lestrade walked quickly towards us, saying; "Good morning, Mr. Holmes, Dr. Watson. I have not touched anything; the victims are also there where they were found. Please come with me."

We walked further down the dark street, leaving the hum of the spectators' voices farther behind us. It was narrow, and hemmed in by the tall buildings on both sides. I fear that even on a sunny day, very little light or warm sunshine would reach down to disturb this miserable alleyway. Unsurprisingly, the air around us smelt damp and mouldy. There imposed itself now, however, a further, penetrating smell, almost metallic, stronger every moment. I knew this dreadful smell all too well; the smell of fresh blood, and the intensity of the aroma told me that it had flown freely. As a doctor, I was no stranger to blood which was present in my work, but this fearful smell brought back other quite different pictures, before my inner eyes.

These were pictures from Afghanistan, pictures of war, pictures of dying comrades with appalling wounds, from which the warm blood, streaming out, soaked into the ground around us. I breathed deeply several times, and tried to banish the images from my mind. I was here to help Holmes, and I forced myself to hold on and go with Holmes and Lestrade to the gruesome scene awaiting us.

All at once I became aware of two bodies, a man and a woman, lying on the ground on their backs, the heads curiously twisted. We took a few steps more, and then we all stopped abruptly before the sight.

The two victims were at once identified. They were Lord Peter Willerby and his wife, Lady Carol, two of the most upright and charitable persons that our time was favoured to know. Here they now lay with their throats cut; and as if that were not enough, there was an even more revolting cut, through their street clothes, running from chest to pelvis. This wound opened their bodies up as to expose a cavity, as the flesh was not simply slashed, but cut so deeply, that stomach and inner organs lay exposed to our sight. So much blood had run out, that it not only covered the lifeless bodies, but left these practically swimming in their own blood. Blood ..., everywhere ...

I felt my stomach turning to water, and my knees giving way. My heart was racing, and I struggled to breathe. Far away, I heard Holmes shout as he called my name. Then all around me went dark.

A sense of burning in my throat, and a fit of coughing, were my first feelings of coming back to the present. I was obviously sitting on a box, while my body was supported by a strong arm around my shoulders. As my eyes opened, I saw that it was Holmes who held me, and who had given me a shot of brandy. His anxious face showed how critically he had watched me.

"Watson, how are you?" he asked.0

"Better", I struggled to say.

"I greatly regret that you were exposed without warning to such an ordeal. But Inspector Lestrade and I both knew what to expect, when we were called to one of these Thames murders. That you had never seen one and were not prepared, was, I fear, our neglect."

"Does that mean," I asked, shocked, as I slowly came back to my senses, "that all the victims had been so horribly mutilated?"

"Yes, Watson, they all carried the same wounds. The press has been told only that they had been brutally murdered. We have deliberately said no more about the precise circumstances of death, because we needed to guard against imitators, which we would have had to distinguish. We are thus able, thanks to this precaution, to say that without any doubt, Lord and Lady Willerby are two further victims of the Thames murderer."

During his remarks, Inspector Lestrade came over to us. "Ah, Doctor Watson, are you feeling better?" he asked kindly. I nodded my answer, which seemed to satisfy him, at which he turned to Holmes. "May I now remove the bodies? I fear that in the meantime not only the bystanders are curious to see something, but also that the rats and flies will not long keep away."

"Oh, yes, thank you, Inspector, I have seen enough," replied Holmes, and turned back to me to continue: "Do you feel well enough to travel back to Baker Street? You will not get a hansom easily around here, but Deptford station is just yards away and the South Eastern Railway has excellent train service into the city, where a cab will be easy to find."

"I think so, but will you not come with me?"

"No, I will now make some further enquiries, and may not be back in Baker Street until this afternoon. If you feel well enough, you may wish to study my newspaper cuttings of the last three weeks, watching out of course for items of interest." I nodded in agreement, and then, with head bowed, spoke quietly to him. "Holmes, I am very sorry that I have been such a disappointment to you. I fear that I am quite useless to you in this matter."

I had scarcely spoken, when his two strong hands took hold of my shoulders and shook me. I looked up at his serious face, as he spoke strongly, but warmly. "Just listen to me, Watson! I am the one who should be reproaching myself! I need your help and loyalty more than ever, and above all I need a friend, one to whom I can, if need be, entrust my life, in implicit, unconditional trust."

I stood up. A feeling of strength and of invincibility suddenly surged through me. "Holmes, I will not disappoint you," I heard myself say, and walked away with a determined step from this dreadful street.

During the journey back to Baker Street, I had time to think of Holmes' moving words. Around the world people admired this extraordinary man and his ability to reason and deduce, but I had just seen into his heart, and that heart was at least as great and embracing as his intelligence.

The Hunt Begins

As soon as I was back in Baker Street, in Mrs. Hudson's care and after a good breakfast, I felt better and was ready to search through Holmes' accumulated newspaper clippings. These covered a variety of public announcements and also private affairs, on the most diverse matters. To illustrate this, I offer two examples. The first was a notice about a forthcoming diamond auction in London, and the other an announcement of a lecture by a Dr. Martens, who was to present to the public his new hair-and-beard colouring elixir. There were lists of ships' arrivals from overseas, death and bereavement notices, reports on unsolved robberies, and offers of, and requests for, contacts for the lonely. I had, I must admit, no idea, under which aspects of his work Holmes might decide what was useful, or indeed not. I searched diligently, but found nothing which might suggest that it was of interest for our enquiries. I was therefore pleased when Holmes reappeared during the afternoon. He had surely discovered something useful, for he revealed it in a facial expression, and in his eyes, as I had so often seen when he was following a possible trail. "Is there anything new?" I asked, eagerly.

Holmes took his place in his armchair, opposite me, and began to speak. "Now, let me begin with the facts as I learned them from Lestrade. The identity of the victims was clear; as you also had seen, they were Lord and Lady Willerby. They had that evening visited a benefit performance at the Elephant and Castle Theatre, held there specially, in a less congenial district, for a charity in which they had a personal interest. After the performance, their coachman could not immediately bring them home, as he found that one wheel of their private coach was damaged. In consequence, the couple took a hansom, which however never arrived at their London residence. Their coachman himself gave the alarm, for when he was finally able, rather later in the night, to drive home, he was advised by the house servants that Lord and Lady Willerby had not yet arrived. Conscious as he was of the Thames murders, he at once informed Scotland Yard, and thus Lestrade came to commit all his available resources to an intensive search. This was concentrated on the districts in which the earlier victims had been found. Within a short time, the hansom cab, which they had taken, was found empty and abandoned. Tracker dogs then took only a short while to discover the bodies. Now, those are the facts, which Lestrade could pass on to me. What do you consider, Watson, are the matters which must stand at the focus of my attention?"

I thought for a moment, and then tried to sound as professional as Holmes. "I consider that these are the matters which should be addressed:

1. Whence came the hansom cab, which was found abandoned?
2. Who was its driver?
3. If he had been attacked, where was the original driver now? Was he murdered too?
4. Why should the hansom go off into this part of dockland, when the Willerbys' London home was far away in a quite different direction?"

"Excellent, Watson! Those were almost exactly the questions I asked myself. And now you shall hear the answers to which my enquiries have led. The hansom was quickly identified. It belonged to the Hansom Cab Central Depot. It had clearly been removed without authority from the fleet of reserve cabs."

"Was the theft already noticed?" I asked.

"No, Watson, it had not been missed, because it had been put on one side for its periodic official examination next week. It was therefore not missed at once."

"But what about the horse? Was that also stolen?" I asked, with some urgency.

"No, Watson, such a theft would immediately be apparent. Our opponents took now a different approach. They went to a livery stable, and a certain Mr. Small hired a cab pony for two days, paying cash on the spot. It was quickly clear that the address left behind by Mr. Small as security was, in fact, spurious, and the description which we have of Mr. Small is so general that it could fit almost any white male member of the British Empire between the ages of 20 and 50."

Holmes paused briefly to stuff his pipe, and so I asked: "Why then did this Mr. Small not also hire a carriage? Surely the theft from the hansom cab depot was a risk?"

"A risk, yes, but not a foolish one. The plans of our opponents required them to take this risk." I did not understand why, and looked at Holmes. "The reason has to be clear, when we consider the kind of vehicles which could be hired in a livery stable." He smiled and continued, "A well-stocked livery stable offers horses and many sorts of vehicles for the carriage of persons and goods. One sort of vehicle, however, they do not offer – a hansom cab. These are all licenced, and must be hired from the Hansom Cab Central Depot".

"That may be, but why did it have to be a hansom?" I asked with impatience.

Holmes looked at me, and asked, "Come, Watson, think about it."

His fingers drummed on the armrest. I endeavoured to ignore this, and suddenly it struck me: "It had to be a hansom cab, so that Lord and Lady Willerby would climb in without suspicion!"

"Just so, Watson, very good! And our last two victims would never on their own initiative have visited the district where they were murdered, so that has to be a most important feature in our enquiries."

"And the driver?" I asked.

"There is no trace of him, nor that he was killed or injured. I therefore conclude that it was his task to bring the potential victims to the scene of the murder. He has therefore to be one of our opponents. The description we have of him is unfortunately no more helpful than that of Mr. Small."

"Holmes, you just spoke of our opponents. Have you a special reason?"

"Yes, my friend, I have indeed. Had these murders been the action of a single person, perhaps of unsound mind, we could have spoken of a guilty one. But in the background of these murders there is something more sinister. This is not a series of indiscriminate murders. Nothing here happens by chance. These crimes are, I now believe, part of something different, something evil and very dangerous. I believe that we are here confronted with a group of completely evil criminals, led by one person, who is just as unscrupulous as the rest but with a clear and intelligent brain, and who has all the actors in his hands."

I was shocked by this declaration, and took time, before I was ready to ask further. "Holmes, if there should really be such a band, responsible for these crimes, what are they intending to do? Why should the victims have been chosen in this way? And why should they be so horribly murdered?"

"I believe, Watson, both the locations and the nature of the murders were deliberately chosen in such an obvious way, distinctively executed, so that they would at once be associated into an identifiable pattern, and thus form a recognisable series."

"But my goodness, Holmes, what was it for?"

"My dear friend, what it is for must still, for us, remain in the dark. But as for the victims – there is, I now have to believe, no connection between them. They were, I fear, taken at random. Our opponents have thereby not only taken victims who work, live or were for other reasons in the district along the Thames. We may fear that the murders are intended to distract from a completely different crime. Or…"

Holmes had closed his eyes, and laid his fingertips together. Much as I would have sought to be party to his thoughts, I knew that I must not disturb him. So it was that we sat silently together, until a knock on the door prefaced the entry of Mrs. Hudson to prepare for supper. I almost expected that our faithful landlady would get a sharp response from Holmes, as she had dared to interrupt him in his thoughts. It was not so. Holmes began to smile to himself, opened his eyes and jumped to his feet. He stepped quickly towards his room, simply saying, "Dear Mrs. Hudson, we need tonight no supper; we have to eat elsewhere." Mrs. Hudson looked at me questioningly, but as I knew no better, I could only shrug my shoulders. Shaking her head and muttering, she cleared the table again, while I hastened to my room and fetched my hat and stick.

A Visit to the Rat and Raven Pub

During the journey, again in a hansom, I soon saw that this was yet another adventurous outing, leading us into a district that Holmes and I might not normally, by choice, have frequented. When I asked where we might be going, Holmes only said, "We are visiting an old acquaintance, Porky Shinwell."

Holmes was obviously not inclined to conversation, and so I was left with my own reflections. I remembered Porky, properly named Shinwell Johnson, who was once a small-scale criminal. Holmes had caught him out, and handed him over to be convicted and sentenced. That had put an end to his mischief. However, after Porky's release from prison, Holmes committed himself, on Porky's behalf, so that he could obtain a license to manage a public house. With this in hand, Porky turned over a new leaf and embarked upon a lawful career, with an honesty which was far removed from the habits of most of his customers. He had never forgotten to whom he owed his new existence, and, though always very careful, was ready to help with such tips and information as he inevitably learned as he kept his ear to the ground. But, goodness, what was the name of his public house?

I was about to ask Holmes as the cab stopped. Holmes climbed out, to go directly to a rather disreputable and dimly lit public house. I followed as quickly as I could to where he opened the door and allowed some light to escape. The sign hanging over the door, which was thus better lit for a moment, let me see the name, in faded lettering: The Rat and Raven. Yes, that was Porky's hostelry, not one of the best, but at least orderly and clean. Holmes was already at the bar, and as I joined him, there came out to greet us a strongly built, suntanned man, with dark wavy hair and a full beard.

"Mr. Holmes and Dr. Watson! What a pleasure to greet you again in my modest house! What can I bring you? How would it be with two tankards of the best beer to be found anywhere in East London?"

"That sounds good, Porky, but I suggest you make it three, and join us," said Holmes with a smile.

"Spoken like the gentleman you are! And would you like something to eat? I've boiled beef and onions, and a steak and kidney pie... For myself, I would take the steak and kidney pie." He crossed his hands before his ample figure. We gladly took his recommendation, and sat at a small corner table where we might talk undisturbed.

As Porky came to us, Holmes came quickly to the subject of the Thames murders. "I fear I cannot tell you much about them that would help you, Mr. Holmes. Naturally, they have troubled us all, here in the East End. I tried a few days ago to find out what was in the air, as I thought you might be interested. It's an affair that seemed to me to be just up your alley. But there was nothing. Mind you, it's not that no one knows anything. Rather, it seemed to me that everyone is afraid even to mention the Thames murders. But I see your glasses are empty; another beer?"

Holmes seemed not to notice his question, so I answered for him. "Thank you, Porky, but don't forget one for yourself."

"Of course, Doctor, I always know the mark of a gentleman." He stepped smartly behind the bar, to return with the three full tankards. As he sat down he suddenly asked, "Mr. Holmes, how were the Thames victims killed?"

I was afraid Holmes might not want to answer, but he spoke quite freely. "With a knife, Porky, but why do you ask?"

"Ah, Mr. Holmes, I was curious, because the newspapers only said that they were brutally murdered."

"Is that really the only reason you ask?" said Holmes, and he seemed to fix him with a penetrating stare. Porky looked deep into his glass, and then breathed heavily. He spoke at first slowly, the words coming cautiously. When he spoke, he looked constantly around, to be sure that no one might be able to hear.

"Mr. Holmes, you are right, there is a reason why I ask. A few days ago, I made the acquaintance of a thoroughly unpleasant person."

"But surely that can often happen in this district?"

"Yes, indeed, Mr. Holmes, but this one was different. And he seemed to be a master with his knife." We looked at one another in some alarm.

Then Holmes spoke, quietly but clearly. "Porky, you tell your stories like Dr. Watson, full of drama, but starting in the middle, or indeed at the end. Please tell me what this was all about. Please tell me everything, from the start, leaving nothing out, even when the details do not seem important."

Porky looked wide-eyed at Holmes, and then he lifted his shoulders and muttered, "I will try, Mr. Holmes."

My friend nodded approvingly, and half closed his eyes, while laying his fingertips together.

"Some two weeks ago, a group of nine rough young men came into the pub. I had not seen them before, and they were so noisy and coarse that they were soon alone in the saloon. This kind of customer, who drives my regulars away, is not

60

welcome here, but what can I do? Disagreeable guests they may have been, but at first they were doing nothing illegal."

"At first?" I asked, "Do you mean that something happened later?"

"You can say that again, Dr. Watson. It began as the door opened and Miss Kitty came in. You have surely heard that she was one of the Thames murder victims." Porky stopped, obviously moved, and then said slowly, "Ladies don't usually come into a pub like this. But then Kitty was no lady, if you see what I mean. But she went straight up to one of the band, and began at once to argue with him loudly."

"Can you describe the man she was talking to", asked Holmes. "What did he look like?"

"From his appearance, he was something better than the others, who were typical thieves and rabble, if you understand. He was in his late twenties, very tall, at least six feet, and had an athletic figure, with black hair, but no beard. That's about it."

"Porky, that was a good description. Do you know what they were arguing about?"

"Not really, Mr. Holmes. But while I was filling the glasses I heard Kitty say something like '*He won't have it, and if I try to get round him again he says he's going to give it all away*'

At that, the athletic one seemed to suggest that Kitty didn't know how to get round him, or that she was perhaps not tempting enough? She flew into a rage, swore at him in words even I wouldn't use, and the next moment he was holding a knife to her neck. That went too far, and I went to separate them. The result was that I was then the one to feel the tip of the knife. Kitty made a jump to reach the door, but that also failed, as our athlete reached under his cloak and drew out two more knives, which he threw quicker than I could see, and pinned Kitty by her wide skirt to the wooden door. Then he looked at me with eyes that were cold and merciless as a fish. His already thin lips narrowed, and I thought that that was it. But one of the others spoke up suddenly, to say, '*Louis, let them go, or you will spoil everything. Think of this evening. Come on now, the Colonel is waiting.'*

"I felt the pressure on my throat relax. Kitty had torn herself free and had already fled. And as the others noisily left my pub, this Louis calmly collected his knives. He turned to throw a few gold coins on the bar and said cynically, *'Forget what you saw, or you won't get to spend that money.'* Then he disappeared, and I closed the door behind him."

For a short moment all was silent. "My goodness, Porky, what an ordeal," I then said completely shocked.

Holmes continued quietly to face Porky and to ask him: "Porky, can you describe the knives?"

"Er, I'm not so sure. They were not your usual knives, and I had never seen them before. But they were very sharp, like the blade of a razor."

"And the gold coins, do you still have them?"

"Why, yes, Mr. Holmes, would you like to see them? I'll just go and fetch them".

While Porky disappeared in the back, Holmes stepped quickly to the pub door and ran his fingers over the woodwork. Taking his magnifying glass, he then examined the door with it again. As Porky returned, he was again sitting at the table, sipping his beer. "Here you are, Mr. Holmes, those are the coins. Are they worth anything?"

Holmes and I each took one, and looked at it carefully. They were French coins, worth little and certainly not gold. "I'm sorry, Porky, they are not. But you said that this all took place about two weeks ago. I don't expect you to remember the exact day…."

"But I do indeed, Mr. Holmes, because I wanted to go that night to the boxing match, the big fight between Ryan and Mell, and that was…"

"On May 22," filled in Holmes unexpectedly.

"But after all this, I didn't feel like it, so I stayed here. But it should have been a great fight, Mr. Holmes, and it was a pity I couldn't go."

"Porky, thank you for being so frank and open. As so often in the past, what you have told me will be a great help. Porky looked at us gratefully. "But I must ask you one last question".

"Yes, Mr. Holmes?"

"Have you told anyone about this?"

"No, Mr. Holmes. When Kitty was found murdered, I thought about going to the police, but with the threats of this Louis in my ears, I didn't dare to. And you know that the death of such a girl doesn't really interest the fine gentlemen at Scotland Yard, so I thought it better to say nothing."

"Good, Porky, and you should do so in future. But I really think it might be better if you were quietly to leave London for a few days. Can you do that?"

"I understand, Mr. Holmes. Thank you for the warning. I've got somewhere I can go for a day or two, destination unknown!"

As soon as we had paid for our beer and dinner, we left the Rat and Raven and soon found a hansom to return to Baker Street.

Reviewing the case

Once we were back in Baker Street, Holmes and I quickly resumed our usual places. I fetched my notebook, and we both found our tobacco. Holmes then started suddenly to talk about the Thames murders.

"Now, Watson, let us try to summarise all the facts we have gathered from Porky. Where shall we start?"

"Perhaps we should first discuss the knife-thrower, Louis."

"Quite right, Watson. The knives, and the way that Porky described them, and my examination of the door, made it clear to me that they were throwing knives, of the type that artists in the circus would use. My question to you as a doctor is then, could such knives be used to create the wounds that the Thames murder victims suffered?"

Yet again, the thought of these dreadful injuries turned over my stomach. I suppressed the feeling, however, to try to

67

consider the injuries professionally, and describe to Holmes my reflections. "The edges of the wounds showed that each one, at the throat and on the body, resulted from a single cut. These cuts were however unusually deep. That suggests a long and a strong knife. The blade must however also be thick and broad enough to avoid breaking under the violence of the attack. I believe, Holmes, that a throwing knife can very well answer this description, and could indeed be the murder weapon."

"Excellent, Watson. Let us then consider Louis as the Thames murderer. What then do we know about him?"

"Porky's description was good, but I fear it might fit many persons in London today. We know however that he is out there with a band of ruffians. He also obviously knew Miss Kitty. Oh, Holmes, if he really is the murderer, then he knew this victim personally. My goodness, such a man must truly be a brutal beast." My own conclusion shocked me, so that I found I was shaking my head in disbelief.

"You are surely right in what you say, Watson, but first let us consider the profession of our Mr. Louis. Porky especially described him as an athlete, and described his agility with his knives. May we then decide that he is a professional knife thrower?" Holmes looked at me significantly.

"Why, Holmes, of course, this Louis is a circus performer!" And then it struck me: "But then it must be easy to catch up with him…"

"Good old Watson, there speaks the man of action! But it is not quite so easy, for I believe that at present no circus is performing in or around London." I looked disappointed at Holmes. "Come, Watson, don't be discouraged, we may not know where Louis is to be found, but I think we do know who he is." I looked at Holmes in amazement. He smiled and continued:

"I think our knife thrower is one Louis Bertrand, 28 years old, and already all too well known in France. The Sûreté has advised me that they are searching for him, because of various serious break-ins and thefts, during which he has not hesitated to commit murder. The Sûreté had already established a connection between these crimes and the locations where a circus stopped for a few days to perform. The thief had never used door or ground floor windows, but always preferred to climb scaffolding and outside walls. Some six weeks ago, they had reached the point where they had enough material to arrest him at the circus. It was a disaster; with his knife-throwing skills, he escaped completely, but I know that the Sûreté lost five experienced officers, of whom two had their throats cut. As you can see, Louis Bertrand is most dangerous, and completely unscrupulous. After his escape he went to ground in the Paris underworld, and the Sûreté thought he was still there. We now, thanks to Porky, know better. Louis Bertrand is in London. Now we have to answer two questions: How, and when, did he get here? And, what is he doing here?"

Holmes broke off and looked at me questioningly. For my part I was already practically speechless. After a moment I said helplessly, "I'm sorry, Holmes, but I don't see how we can answer either of them."

"Well, Watson, we do know something. Let us look at the known facts:

1. Louis Bertrand had to flee from the French police in great haste.
2. He would have had to give up his wages and also the goods or wealth he had stolen, so he is practically without means
3. The established bands of criminals in Paris will not touch him, as he represents, after the police murders, too high a risk.
4. Bertrand appears in Porky's pub, with various partners, and seems to have still some French money."

"I consider that these facts allow of only one conclusion. There is here in London a criminal, who has need of the accomplishments of M. Bertrand. He has procured for Bertrand forged papers, and ensured that he could travel to London. In return, Bertrand has rendered him a first service, in that he has committed the Thames murders."

"Holmes, you are now speaking as though these murders are only a part of whatever Bertrand will have to do for this unknown criminal. How do you arrive there? Were the Thames murders not bad enough?"

"Indeed, Watson, these murders were gruesome enough, but do recall that they might only have been staged as part of a much bigger, more far-reaching plot. The murder series could itself have been committed by any one of a number of hired London murderers. It did not necessarily require a Louis Bertrand to carry them out. No, I believe that there is a greater crime being planned, for which also his acrobatic climbing skills are needed."

"But for what, then, might such a murder series serve, Holmes?"

"We may consider, as I said, that they were perhaps a diversion, but another possibility is that a certain person was indeed to be murdered, and that the other murders only serve to cover up that crime which was part of a real premeditated, purpose." I stared at Holmes in disbelief, but he continued unperturbed, "The next question has then to be, which victims were only the cover, and which one was really the object?"

"Have you then already a suspicion, who it might have been?"

"I tend to think that the person really aimed at was Lord Willerby, especially as Porky led us back to May 22."

"I recall," I asked, "that Porky had remembered that day, when he had his own experience with Bertrand. But how does that bring us to Lord Willerby?" I was confused, and looked to Holmes for clarification. Some time elapsed, before he replied carefully:

"Watson, what I am about to tell you must not be repeated outside these walls. I have been asked by Mycroft to investigate the theft from the Warehouse of Tucker and Sons, which, as you may recall, took place on the night of May 22."

"Yes, indeed, Holmes, I do remember now. I read of it in the newspaper cuttings. The robbery was certainly a most daring affair, as the thieves appear to have entered by a roof window, and then afterwards taken the stolen goods on a wagon waiting outside. But what is so special, Holmes, that one robbery, in itself not unusual, should interest Mycroft? And why must it remain so secret?"

While I spoke, Holmes had sunk his head and stared at the floor. Now he looked directly at me, and said, in a penetrating voice, "Because this is not an everyday robbery. The thieves took away twenty boxes of dynamite."

Appalled, my mouth wide open, I had to hear the rest. "As I was a few days incognito in the docks, I tried to pick up the trail of the dynamite. There was nothing, so whoever has the dynamite now has not attempted to offer it for sale. But can you imagine what destructive power this dynamite possesses? But now listen carefully. Her Majesty is expecting next month the visit of a number of heads of state to resolve certain outstanding questions of foreign policy. The arrangements for this meeting were entrusted to none other than Lord Willerby. Mycroft anticipates a possibility that radical forces might take advantage of this meeting to organise assassination attempts."

Still speechless, I tried to come to terms with all this new information. Holmes continued to explain: "In the newspapers, the robbery was played down. Nothing was said about the contents of the boxes, and it was also not reported that several men were guarding them."

"What became of the watchmen," I asked, although I had an unpleasant feeling that I already knew the answer.

"They were murdered, their throats cut."

"Great God, Holmes, this was then surely Bertrand, the more so as the thieves came over the roof."

"Yes, Watson, I think so too".

"Holmes, if I have properly understood this, there is then, here in London, a criminal, who has so far been able:

1. To bring Bertrand to Britain
2. To arrange a series of brutal murders
3. To steal a strongly guarded store of dynamite
4. To plan an attack on visiting heads of state

"For goodness' sake, Holmes, what can it be? Is it the ominous Colonel, of whom they were talking in Porky's pub?"

"No, Watson, if, as I am already convinced, the 'Colonel' is Colonel Sebastian Moran, of whom I am already well-aware, then the brain in the background is Professor Moriarty."

"And do you know him personally?"

"Yes, Watson. Professor Moriarty has a chair of mathematics at one of our lesser universities. He had an outstanding publication on the Binomial Theorem some years ago, which attracted much favourable attention in those circles. He had an excellent reputation, and is above all reproach. It was up to now never possible to pin anything on him, and yet I know that he is the mastermind behind any number of serious crimes. The Professor and I have on various occasions run up against one another, but he has always countered my efforts. He is outstandingly clever, and his good fortune still holds. But I promise you, Watson, that I will lay low this Napoleon of crime, even if it is at the cost of my life. It would be worth it."

Suddenly shocked, I looked at my friend. He seemed to be looking far away, but as he realised my distress he smiled and said, "Don't look so alarmed, Watson, we are not there yet. And if the moment were near, I would surely not give up without a struggle. But now, Watson, it is time to sleep. You look very drawn."

"And you must sleep too, Holmes," I replied.

"Yes, indeed, but later. First I must send two telegrams, one to Lestrade and one to my friends at the Sûreté. They should also be aware that Monsieur Bertrand is in London."

Answers, but More Questions

Holmes' description of these terrifying events all around us, and his portrayal of a fearsome scenario before us, were enough to keep me awake a long time, and had I not been truly exhausted, I would scarcely have slept. Before waking I vaguely saw fragments of dreams in which Holmes and I were in a labyrinth and desperately sought a way out. As I awoke, a glance at the clock told me it was indeed ten o'clock; I washed and dressed quickly, and knocked on Holmes' door. There was no reply. The living room was also empty, so I called Mrs. Hudson. She told me that Mr. Holmes had left early without breakfast, but had instructed her not to wake me. She shortly appeared again with a breakfast tray, and I saw that the post had brought a letter for me. As I saw the familiar handwriting, my heart beat faster in happy anticipation. It was a letter from my dear Mary. She wrote:

Dearest John,

Mrs. Forrester and I are enjoying a happy time together. We laugh a lot, and have also gone out together. On the coming Saturday evening we will see Shakespeare's play 'A Midsummer Night's Dream' performed in the Royal Park at Greenwich. You will remember how I love this play. So that it has the authentic atmosphere, a small amphitheatre is being built in the Park. The tickets were limited in number, and quickly sold out, but Mrs. Forrester was able to obtain two tickets on the grandstand. As you see, I am well able to enjoy myself, even though I miss you all the time.

I hope your enquiries are making progress, so that the criminals can soon be brought to justice. Take good care of yourself, my dearest, and please give my greeting to Mr. Holmes.

Love,
Mary.

I miss you too, my dear, I thought, as I read the letter a second time after breakfast. I had just folded it again, when Holmes returned, bursting into our living room. "Ah, Watson, how good that you have already risen, and, as I see, you have already breakfasted. Did you sleep better in this night?"

"I think so, but at least I have slept longer, which must be good after all our excitement. But how is it with you, Holmes?"

"Ah, Watson, you know that when a case occupies all my faculties, I minimise my other needs."

"Yes, that I know all too well, but sometimes you must take time to restore your strength. You have a strong constitution and an iron will, but if you don't take care, you will one day suffer for it."

Here, with these last words, it was not only the troubled friend, but also the doctor, who spoke. The ruthless demands which Holmes made on his body were something I could not condone. He looked at me seriously and said, "I value your concern, Watson, but how are we to solve this case without investigations?" I had of course no answer, and scarce opportunity to reflect, before Holmes said suddenly, "But you would surely like to know where I was, so early in the morning?"

"Naturally, Holmes!"

"Good, then I will tell you while we are on the way."

"On the way?"

"Yes, Watson, a hansom is waiting downstairs. I must make further urgent enquiries, but I did not want to do so without you. So now, come along, please" With these words he hurried to the stairs, and I took up quickly my hat and stick to follow him.

As we sat together in the hansom, Holmes explained that he had already visited Mycroft, to learn more about Lord Willerby. "Concerning the requirements of our Foreign Policy, a successor has already been found," he explained.

"Do you know who it is?"

"Yes, it is Lord Cavendish, who will be officially named next week. His political orientation corresponds perfectly to that of Lord Willerby. He will also take all responsibility for the planned meeting of heads of state."

"But Holmes, if Lord Willerby was really the intended victim, then his murder has achieved nothing?"

"Quite, Watson, everything is as before, except that Lord Cavendish will now have special protection."

"But would that not mean perhaps that all the victims of the Thames murder, even from the viewpoint of the murderers, were meaninglessly killed?"

"Yes, Watson, I fear it might be so. Unless, of course, the real target was not Lord Willerby, but another person."

I looked at Holmes in surprise. "But who could that then be?"

"That I do not yet know, Watson, but before today is out, we will attempt to get to the bottom of that secret at least".

"Where then do we begin?"

"We will start first with a visit to Brown and Co. They build, and also rebuild, wagons and carriages of all kinds, and effect first-class repairs. Why, do you think, are we going there?"

"I think I understand. We will hope to find here the defective coach of the Willerby household, and you will establish whether the defective wheel had been maliciously damaged."

"Splendid, Watson, and I see that we are already there. Driver, will you please wait here? We will not be long".

Mr. Brown was a reliable, earnest and helpful man. He confirmed that the damaged coach had been brought to him, and since, under the circumstances, there could at present be no instructions for the repair, he had placed it in storage. It would there remain safe until the Willerby family's affairs were cleared up, when they would surely come to give instructions. It was naturally in order, that we might see the coach. Should we need help, we had only to ask, and with this Mr. Brown left us to carry on with his other tasks. Holmes examined, first with the naked eye and then with his magnifying glass, the spokes. Then he looked more closely at the damaged part. As he finished, I asked him what he thought.

"The splintered wood is really quite conclusive, Watson. Without a doubt a material weakness in the wood, material fatigue, and a mishap no more than a week earlier, involving a near collision with a cart, led to the defect. Manipulation or sabotage can therefore definitely be excluded."

"Really, Holmes," I replied, "I can understand how you identified the weakness in the wood, and the material fatigue, but how would you know that there had been a near-collision with a cart a week earlier?"

"Here, Watson, just look at these light scratches at the rear of the coach. The height means that the contact could only have been with a cart, but as the scratches are shallow, it cannot have been a real collision. It is indeed probable that the Willerby coachman did not even notice."

"That seems likely, Holmes. But what makes you so sure that the incident was only a week earlier?"

"Lestrade had told me that the coachman is a most conscientious, reliable and thorough person. Had he observed the scratch, he would certainly have dealt with it at once; it was, after all, not deep. This tells me, as you will see, Watson, that he was unaware of the contact with the cart. On cleaning the coach, however, he would surely have seen it. The present cleanliness of the coach, and the reliability of the coachman, both together tell me that the scratch occurred after he last cleaned the coach, and that can surely not be more than a week beforehand." As was so often the case, Holmes made his conclusions seem a natural consequence of his review of the individual facts. I, however, never failed to be impressed by these demonstrations of combination and deduction. "Have you any questions, Watson?" he now asked.

"Not on this aspect" I replied, "But does this all mean that Lord and Lady Willerby were indeed arbitrary victims?"

"Quite, Watson, and with this conclusion we must come back to our starting question. Which of the murdered persons was the intended victim?" "Perhaps John Miller. He worked in the docks; perhaps there is a link between him and the theft of the dynamite at Tucker and Sons?"

"A first-rate idea, Watson." I looked at him with some satisfaction. "I also had this idea after the theft of the dynamite. But after I had spent some days looking into the matter, I had to conclude that there was no such connection."

My glance at Holmes betrayed my disappointment. "Come, your conclusion was nevertheless fully logical. Just keep it up, and we will consider which of the remaining victims might be the one we seek."

"I think we might consider the insurance clerk, Samuel Williams."

"And why do you suggest him?"

"Because I know that Lloyds is involved in insuring all kinds of things. They might have had a policy to cover the dynamite, so that Williams may have known about it."

"That is surely a good idea, Watson, and one we will have to follow up in any case. And what can we say of the other victims?"

"I don't know, Holmes. We have still the nurse, Sophia Walter. But what connection can there be between her and the theft of dynamite?" Holmes looked thoughtful, so I went on. "The same might also be said of the girl, Kitty. She was most probably killed after the argument in Porky's pub."

Holmes was still indecisive, and then asked, "And what about Nathaniel Cook?"

"I think he was simply unfortunate, because he was with Kitty. He had perhaps tried to help Kitty, just as Porky had done, and it cost him his life."

"Yes, Watson, that is certainly possible; but I would in any case like to visit the place where he worked. As he had no family, all that I have up to now been able to learn about him came from his landlady."

During this conversation, we had reached the waiting hansom. Holmes gave the driver the next destination, which was Greenwich, the Royal Park.

As we began the journey, I asked Holmes something which had been troubling me for some time. "Holmes, we have up to now worked in the expectation that there is a connection between the theft of the dynamite, and one of the Thames murder victims. What if this proves not to be so?"

It was a while before Holmes answered. Then he said quietly, "In that case, my dear friend, we start again at the beginning."

We remained silent for the rest of the journey, but these words hung heavily over us in our hansom as we sat there.

More Investigations

On arrival at Greenwich Park, we left our cab with an instruction to the driver to wait for us as before. It was a busy scene, because on this evening the performance, of "A Midsummer Night's Dream," was to take place. For this purpose a replica amphitheatre of wood and sailcloth had been built. It had a most convincing atmosphere, and I could well imagine that Mary and Mrs. Forrester would truly enjoy the evening's entertainment. We asked our way of one of the workpeople, who invited us to follow him.

He brought us to a gentleman of some 60 years, sparse hair, stocky, but with a rather unhealthy-looking red face. Before we could introduce ourselves, he had already announced himself as Charles Havendale, and declared himself impressed at our initiative, coming personally to buy tickets, but no, regrettably all was sold out, and he could not help us. As he stopped for a moment, apparently to draw breath, we seized the chance to introduce ourselves, and to explain why we were there. At first Mr. Havendale looked at us in surprise, and then he started again, as vigorously as before.

"Ah, yes, Nathan, that was a good man. You could rely on him. It was at once obvious that he had once been a soldier, and surely a downright good one. He was always the first here, and the last to leave. He supervised the work on this curious theatre. In spite of his leg injury, an old war wound, he would crawl about, even under the sailcloth here, and assure himself that the wooden construction was properly executed according to the plans. Truly, I wouldn't have known where to find another one like him."

I observed that this endless flood of words annoyed Holmes, for people who could not answer his questions directly, or who wandered off the subject, simply fatigued him. He broke in: "Then the death of Mr. Cook must certainly have been a blow to you?"

Mr. Havendale looked up sharply. "It was indeed! And please do not think me to be without respect, because Nathan's death has personally moved me deeply. But you can also understand that with having to have this whole infernal construction ready for this evening, his death was also an immediate catastrophe."

In order to interrupt Mr. Havendale's discourse, I risked another question. "But it seems that you have achieved your object, for all seems to be almost ready? It makes a very good impression."

"Indeed it does, sir, and you would not guess how much time, planning and work go into such a project. The normal guest will simply enjoy it and not give a thought to the difficulties and problems that must be overcome. If it wasn't for Leo, a colleague of Nathan, who came forward, I don't know where we would have been. That young man was, thank goodness, as capable as Nathan was. Nothing was too much for him, and he also took on the job of watchman, for the safety of the theatre in the night hours."

"Then you must have been very pleased to have found such a workman," countered Holmes. Might I perhaps meet him, for he seems to have been very valuable, this Mr. – what was his name? – and I can ask him also about his dead friend, Mr. Cook?"

"His name is Leo Baxter. But you can no longer speak with him here, because Benson and Co, the building company in Brighton, have poached him from me, and I understand that he left only this morning for Brighton, where from Monday morning he will be employed to execute urgent repairs to the Marine Parade. I fear I do not yet know where he is lodging there."

"Perhaps, then, Mr. Havendale, you can still help us in one further matter?"

"Of course, sir, as far as it is in my power".

Before we were treated to a speech in favour of helpfulness in general, and his own in particular, Mr. Havendale found Holmes continuing with his question. "You surely know that on the day that Mr. Cook died, he had been in the company of a certain Miss Kitty. Do you know anything about this friendship?"

Mr. Havendale's complexion turned slightly redder, and he hastened to say, "Of Nathan's private life I can truly say very little. He was a widower and had no children. I think that young woman might have been a kind of compensation for both, if you understand…"

As Holmes looked on quietly, as if waiting for an explanation, Mr. Havendale glanced up at us almost conspiratorially. "My goodness", he muttered, "There are times when a man needs a woman….."

To save Mr. Havendale from further embarrassment, I asked him quickly, "Is there anything you would like to add?"

"No, sir, I think there is nothing more."

"Then I must thank you for being so helpful, Mr. Havendale," replied Holmes. With this he turned to me and said, "Now, Watson, we must continue our enquiries."

It was already afternoon as we arrived at the Royal Exchange, the impressive building between Cornhill and Threadneedle Street, where Lloyds of London had its offices, and Lord Penling was ready to receive us. Holmes gave his visiting card to the porter, and we soon found ourselves in a substantial and generously appointed office. Facing us was a handsome and well-dressed man approaching fifty years of age. This was Lord Graham Penling, who as a board member was known to conduct the affairs of Lloyds most correctly and honourably. His greeting was friendly, and he was prepared to talk at once about the former employee, the late Samuel Williams.

"Of course I will help you, if I possibly can. I was told of your investigation. What would you like to know?"

"First of all, My Lord, I would like to know, in view of the audacious robbery of the 20 boxes which were stored there, whether the warehouses of Tucker & Sons were insured by you against theft."

"Yes, Mr. Holmes, that is so."

"Thank you, Lord Penling. Did you or anyone else at Lloyds know what the contents of these boxes might be?"

"No, Mr. Holmes, we do not need to know this, because Tucker & Sons use these storerooms only for confidential requirements of the government. As there is in this situation no problem of the good faith of the insured party, the insurance policy with Tucker & Sons is an all-inclusive arrangement regardless of the goods themselves actually stored there. In the case of such a theft we pay a fixed amount of £1000."

"My next question must then be, did Mr. Williams have any professional interest in this all-in policy?"

"No, Mr. Holmes, not at all, as he was engaged in a quite different sector of our business, handling insurance claims for sea-going ships lost or in distress."

"Had he then, my Lord, connections overseas?" I asked, thus bringing a question on a suspicion which had begun to occupy me.

"Certainly, Dr. Watson, for we insure ships on the seven seas and under many flags. The insurance business is truly international."

I could hardly wait to discuss my idea with Holmes, and looked at him eagerly. He, however, was obviously also preparing to leave. "Then I think, Lord Penling, that that is all that we needed to ask you. Thank you indeed, My Lord, for the time and care you have given us."

We were escorted most courteously out of the office, to where a porter was present to lead us to the street door. As we climbed into our hansom, which again we had instructed to wait for us, Holmes gave the driver the next address, 221b Baker Street.

During our journey home, I shared with Holmes my suspicions. Mr. Williams had regular contacts abroad. It could have been possible for him to locate Monsieur Bertrand, then hiding from justice in France, with an offer of a voyage to England. Organising the voyage would not have presented any great problems. There came to this thought then another, which also offered a reason for Mr. Williams to have been involved. We knew that he had regularly attended illegal rat-baiting matches, and placed bets. He may have had other gambling interests, but in any case, as a gambler he would always have a need for ready money. Might this background not have made him a candidate for blackmailing?"

Holmes said nothing during my description of these ideas. Although his eyes were half closed, I knew that he was following closely. At the end he reflected for a while before speaking: "Watson, you have introduced one or two most interesting considerations, and we will have to come back to them. But today we will not achieve much more, I think it is now time to sit in our familiar surroundings, with good tobacco, and reflect on all that we have learned so far. Do you agree, old friend?"

"Certainly, Holmes."

The journey continued in silence, each of us occupied with his own thoughts. I was somewhat satisfied that I had, as Holmes had confirmed, been able to deliver useful contributions to solving this truly complex crime. I sat back reassured in my seat, and there grew in me the conviction that it would not be long before we knew what the learned Professor Moriarty was planning. I had thus not the least suspicion, how soon and in what a dreadful way, my feeling would become reality.

The Fog Clears a Little

As we were back in Baker Street, Mrs. Hudson brought us a belated afternoon tea, and Holmes poured us a sherry. We again took up our places on either side of the chimneypiece, and Holmes adopted his cross-legged position in his armchair, before filling his pipe. Before long he would sink into his thoughts, and then I never dared to interrupt him, so I took the opportunity to ask a question which was greatly troubling me.

"Holmes, may I ask you something?"

"Of course, my dear friend, what is it?"

"I would dearly like to know what Professor Moriarty might be intending to do with all the stolen dynamite."

"Well, yes, that is the most fundamental question, Watson, and it occupies me the whole time. Believe me, I would be much more at ease, if only I had an answer. I can at present only give you two possibilities, both unsatisfactory. Would they interest you?"

"I would be pleased if you would share them with me, Holmes."

"My first suspicion was that he is planning one or more political attacks at the forthcoming meeting. This was supported by the fact that as far as we know the explosives are still completely in his possession. Where could he otherwise use such a quantity?"

"Mm, that sounds convincing."

"Perhaps, Watson, but it does not satisfy me. I am not happy about it."

"Why not, then?

"Because Professor Moriarty is a master of tactics. His ability, his brilliance, by which he is able to lead his criminal world, depends on structures, rules and processes which are, in essence, logical. Now, however, look at the world of politics. You had in your book 'A Study in Scarlet' already described how I claim no great qualities in that field, but one thing is clear to me: In politics many of the things that happen cannot be justified by logic; they are emotional. I find it difficult to believe that Professor Moriarty, a master tactician who values logic in all his dealings, would take an initiative in that field."

"But what then is your second option, Holmes?"

"It was, that Moriarty intends to use the dynamite for a serious theft. That is much more in keeping with his nature. The quantity that he has stolen is enough to break into every building and to open every safe."

"Holmes, you may be right; the idea has certainly much to speak for it."

"Yes, Watson, I know, and yet I am still not happy about it."

"Oh, why not?"

"Because a large-scale burglary with dynamite would at once be far too obvious, and most destructive. Before the thieves could get their booty out of the building, they would already be arrested. Such a plan must fail. To do it, he would have to render the whole police force ineffective. And how would he do that?"

Indeed, I thought, if Holmes has no better answer, then neither had I. I looked at him again, but saw that we would get no further now, for his eyes were closed and his fingertips were together, as he thought about the case. For a while I followed my own thoughts, but then fetched my notebook to record the outcome of our most recent enquiries.

Shortly after six o'clock there was a knock on the living room door, and Mrs. Hudson came in. She announced Inspector Lestrade, who had hoped to find us. I looked doubtfully at Holmes, who hated to be disturbed when he was thinking. But all was well, as he had opened his eyes and asked

Mrs. Hudson to bring in the Inspector, while he asked me to pour out another sherry.

Lestrade was still very nervous, but at least he seemed a little more composed than before, as I noted by his stronger, clearer voice on greeting us.

"Good evening, Mr. Holmes, Doctor Watson. I would like to thank you for the information you have given me, that the Thames murderer may in fact be this Louis Bertrand."

"Have you found any trace of him yet, Inspector?" I asked eagerly.

"Regrettably not, Doctor Watson, and I must admit that I am far from happy to know that such an unscrupulous killer may now be on the loose in my city. But for the moment it is a most valuable start, for with your news, I at least have a suspect to put before the Commissioner and the public."

I could readily imagine what he felt. The hysterical mood in the city was already reaching grotesque proportions, and the pressure upon Lestrade to produce results must have been very burdensome. I was relieved that we had helped him, at least this far. I said so to him. "That must already be a weight off your shoulders, Inspector. And this Bertrand must come to light somewhere soon."

"I most heartily hope so, Dr. Watson. The search is on, and now I can only wait."

"Then perhaps you can take time this weekend to enjoy some calm. It would be good for you if you could relax." Here, of course, it was again the doctor in me who spoke.

"Doctor, you are most thoughtful, but there will be no rest for me today or tomorrow."

"Oh, and why is that, Inspector?" He had made me curious.

"But surely," he said, "You know about the great Shakespeare performance tonight in Greenwich's Royal Park?"

"Yes, I do, but what then?"

"Well, the Commissioner has made clear that it will go badly with me if there is any trouble, like another Thames murder. That means, in simple words, that we have already positioned a major body of police to ensure the safety of all the streets between the Park and the Thames."

"My goodness! Then you certainly have a busy night ahead of you."

"That is surely so. And on Monday there is the diamond auction. The diamonds to be sold, some of the world's finest, are to be transported tomorrow morning from the Bank of England to the auction house of Christies. And you will not be surprised to learn, that my men and I are responsible, naturally, for the safety of the transfer." Lestrade certainly looked burdened by all that he had to do, and I felt a moral responsibility to express to him my sympathy. We both looked towards Holmes, and awaited his comments. During Lestrade's description he had kept his eyes closed and seemed almost to be asleep. Since he had up to now said nothing, and had in any case hardly slept the previous night, I feared that he was completely exhausted. But then, suddenly, he opened his eyes, jumped up and threw his pipe aside. His eyes blazed.

"My God, Watson, Lestrade, I have it! I know what Professor Moriarty intends to do, and it is, I have to declare, a completely unscrupulous and villainous plan."

Lestrade looked up, completely surprised, and could only say, "Who is Professor Moriarty?"

Holmes paced backwards and forwards, with great rapid strides from wall to wall, confirming his own thoughts, muttering to himself until he uttered a loud "Yes, of course."

I turned to Lestrade. "Professor Moriarty is a mastermind among criminals. Holmes thinks that he is behind the Thames murders and also the theft of dynamite, and that he has a much bigger criminal plan in preparation."

"Just a minute, Doctor, what is this about a theft of dynamite? When and where was that? And just what are we talking about?"

I had quite forgotten, that this was a matter of complete secrecy. I searched for a suitable answer, but Holmes spoke up now with a new authority. "That need not now concern us, Inspector. Much more important is that a large load of dynamite is now in London, and I know now that Professor Moriarty intends to use it against us all. Now, Lestrade, you must dispatch two teams. One will go to the Bank of England and prevent Moriarty´s band from blowing up the safes and cleaning out the diamonds".

"But, Holmes," I interjected, "you have already said that the police would have to be distracted."

"Quite, Watson."

"But we have police patrolling between Greenwich Park and the Thames. Are they then no help?" I was afraid that Holmes had made a logical error, but it was of course not so.

"Watson, that is quite right, the police patrol there is of no significance. It is the park itself which concerns us."

He turned back to Lestrade and continued: "You must at once send a second body of police to Greenwich Park."

Lestrade had understandably failed to follow the conversation between Holmes and myself, and asked, "Might I ask what my men are expected to do there?"

Holmes now tolerated no questions, but said peremptorily, "If they get there in time they will prevent an attack with dynamite on the amphitheatre which there awaits its distinguished guests. If they are not in time, they can attend to the dead and injured."

As Holmes spoke these last words, I suddenly lost all awareness of where I was. Mary, my beloved Mary, was to be there, at that performance. I could not hold back a tortured groan, and in an indescribable pain my mouth formed words I could scarcely speak, Oh, my God, Mary, No! My pulse was racing, and I gasped for breath, as icy fingers seemed to tighten round my heart.

In Greenwich Park

Although years have gone by since we heard Holmes make this awful prediction, my pen still shakes in my hand as I write these lines. After my cry of shock, Holmes and Lestrade had looked up sharply at one another. Holmes hastened to me and put his strong hands on my shoulders, all this I learned later, for I was in panic, paralysed by fear, unable to see or hear. It was only when I felt Holmes' energetic grip that I began to come back gradually to an awareness of where I was. Now I heard his urgent voice, searching a way into my consciousness. "Watson, Watson, can you hear me? What is with Mary?"

He used her Christian name deliberately to break into my thoughts. It worked, and now I was able to describe my fear. At first I spoke disjointedly, as is often the case with those who suffer shock. "Holmes, Oh, my God! Holmes, Mary will be killed, she and Mrs. Forrester are attending the Shakespeare performance; she will be there, in the park, in the grandstand...."

As I tried to speak, I fixed Holmes with a rigid stare. As I knew him well, I could see how his eyes narrowed, and his lips were pressed together to a narrow slit, revealing how my words had shaken his usual calm. Then his clarity of reasoning took over again, repressing every trace of emotion, so that, as was now necessary, he could think and act for us both.

"Come, Watson, we are not yet beaten. We will not wait for a police escort, but take a hansom and go at once to Greenwich and the park."

"And I will mobilise every policeman I can find," added Lestrade energetically, as he drained his sherry glass. We all went through the narrow hallway and to the stairs, leaving a mystified Mrs. Hudson.

Holmes and Lestrade looked in vain on the street for a free hansom. They found none, so Lestrade determined to commandeer two cabs, stepping out into the path of a cab horse and obliging the driver to stop, before showing his warrant card and saying to the driver and his indignant passengers, with clear authority, "In the name of Her Majesty and of the Law, in my capacity at Scotland Yard, I am taking this vehicle……"

I heard no more as Holmes suddenly turned to me and said, "Watson, I think it good to bring your revolver." Relieved to be able again to act, I ran upstairs, into my bedroom, and took my Army revolver from its drawer where it lay ready. As I prepared to run down again, I heard Mrs. Hudson ask, urgently, what it was all about. There was no time to explain, but she showed so much pain and concern in her face that I called out, over my shoulder, "We have to save hundreds of lives, including perhaps Mary's."

The good woman was speechless. But as I left by the street door, I heard a clear voice, calling, "I will pray for you all".

Lestrade, before he commandeered a second cab to go to warn his police colleagues, charged our driver against threat of penalty, to take the most direct way to Greenwich. Our cab raced through the streets. We were at first silent, but then, as we came nearer, Holmes spoke to determine how we should proceed.

"Watson. I think we first seek out the theatre manager responsible for the performance. Lestrade will contact his colleagues in the Royal Parks Police. We must prevent use of the word 'dynamite' in public, for a mass panic could only help Professor Moriarty to achieve his objects."

"Yes, Holmes, the director will be behind the stage."

"Very good, Watson, I will speak to him, and you will search for your wife and bring her, as soon as you find her, away from here. Should we lose contact with one another, we will meet again, I hope fit and strong, in Baker Street."

While Holmes went his way, I raced to the entrance of the amphitheatre, where the performance had already started, and looked searchingly up and down the rows. It took time to find Mary, but then I located her, in the middle of the top row of seats, Although Mrs. Forrester should have been there with her, I could find her nowhere. The rows of seats could be reached from two side staircases. I took that on the right, and ran up to the top, my view fixed on Mary. Suddenly there was silence. Had the warning come in time? The actors' voices ceased, and I could now hear only the voice of one man on the stage. It was the director of the production, who spoke clearly, to announce that the performance would be stopped. He explained briefly of a warning of an approaching severe thunderstorm, which obviously puzzled many guests who only saw a mild, warm summer evening. With his assurance, however, of a repeat performance as soon as possible, with full validity of tickets, and with the police at hand to organise an orderly evacuation of the theatre, the guests started to leave their seats. This meant that they stood up and began to move towards the exits, and I was now trying to make my way against this crowd to where Mary had been sitting. Inevitably I lost sight of her. Calling for her was useless, as everyone was talking as they moved. When, however, I then had a clear view of the top row of seats, I had to admit with alarm that she was no longer there. Since she had not come down the steps on my side, she had presumably gone down on the other side, farther away. I turned on my heel and let the crowd carry me down again. Once at the bottom, I made my way through the crowd, to get to the far side of the amphitheatre. My heart was still hammering wildly, but then I saw Mary, and ran to greet her.

"Mary, Mary!" I called, and in a moment I held her in my arms and pressed her to me. Then, taking a step back, I held her face in my hands and caressed her.

Delight, but also astonishment, were in her eyes, as she suddenly asked, "But, John, why are you here?"

"Mary, there is no time for explanations, but believe me, you must leave the park at once. Where is Mrs. Forrester?"

Mary looked at me in complete surprise and answered, "Mrs. Forrester twisted her ankle this afternoon, and was so unable to be at the performance. I offered to stay with her, but she would not hear of it, and so I came alone."

While she was explaining, I had taken her by the hand and was going to the exit. Here a man suddenly burst into view, apparently from underneath the stands, and he was running with his head down. He bumped into us, so abruptly that we almost fell. He staggered back, and then seemed to catch himself, to land squarely on his two feet. As he did so, his cape fell open, and I felt again a panic take hold, at the sight that met my eyes, for across his chest was a broad leather belt, a halter for five wicked throwing knives. This man – he could only be Louis Bertrand, the Thames murderer himself! I looked at him shocked, and the word escaped, "Bertrand".

In the same moment I realised my mistake, for now Bertrand knew that, while thinking to get clean away, he had been recognised. Mary and I were now a threat to him, for we had seen and recognised him, Louis Bertrand, the Thames murderer, here, apparently escaping from the planned scene of the crime. My inner eye saw again the fearfully savaged bodies of Lord and Lady Willerby. I had to move fast to save Mary from that fate. A step to the left, and I pulled Mary behind me, while I never took my eyes off him. Porky was right, his eyes were cold as a fish, betraying no feeling. As he studied me, he realised that I was protecting Mary with my body, and a cynical smile came to his lips. He spoke coldly: "I'm sorry, Madame, but your friend is too inquisitive and I can take no risks".

I made a grab for my jacket pocket, and my fingers closed over my revolver butt, but I had no chance to draw it out, for in that moment one of Bertrand's throwing knives penetrated my lower arm. A flash of intolerable pain was made worse, in that my arm no longer obeyed me. Mary screamed and rushed to my side. A few theatregoers were still going past, but they seemed to notice nothing of the threatening tragedy. Mary stared incredulously at the knife still in my arm, and at that moment came the next fearful, penetrating pain in my right leg. Bertrand had thrown another knife into my thigh. It gave way, helpless, beneath me, and I fell back on the floor. I again heard Mary's scream, and then how she called my name as she knelt beside me. Bertrand seemed to take pleasure at the situation, for, through my pain, I heard his scornful laugh. I was losing control, but through the veil, which seemed to fall over my eyes, I tried to keep Mary in view. Tears rolled down her face, and over her cheeks. We seemed to be at the mercy of a bestial creature who enjoyed playing with death. I saw how he took another knife, and I tried to roll away, but it was useless, I was too weak, but then, just in that moment, from the grandstand, a lean, dark figure threw himself down, panther-like, on Bertrand. It was Holmes, who had mounted the grandstand, had seen us and so fell on Bertrand. Now both men struggled to control the knife in Bertrand's hand. Holmes' presence gave me new strength. But I was losing too much blood; an artery in my leg had been cut. It must be bound, and I told Mary, "Quick, listen to me. You must bind my leg."

"How do I do that?"

"Tear out a large piece of your petticoat." I had hardly got the words out, as she did so and looked at me. "Fold it together and bind it round my leg just above the wound."

"Like this?"

"Yes, that is just right. Now make a knot and pull the ends as tight as you can. Never mind if I shout, you must pull as hard as you can."

As I groaned with the pain, she was shocked and let go a little. "You must pull it really tight", I insisted, and this time she nodded and pulled it tighter again. Then she closed her eyes and tied a firm knot in the fabric. Now I could look up. "Thank you; that is good." I whispered, and I saw the exhaustion in her face.

But where were the others? I saw that Holmes had taken the knife that might have been for me, for Bertrand's belt was empty, but now both of them held a knife and were trying to find a way through one other's defense, without giving any opening. It was like a macabre dance, with rapid thrusts in between. I realised that Holmes was losing strength, but it was not that he lacked stamina. He had been wounded, and I saw on his sleeve a dark patch of blood, which was growing rapidly. The loss of blood must weaken him. Bertrand drove Holmes further back, and he would soon have no more chance to avoid the attacks. Then Bertrand would give him a fatal wound. Again I saw the bodies of Lord and Lady Willerby. I must help Holmes, but my strength failed. Was this to be the end of us all? Mary saw and understood. She grasped the hopelessness in a moment.

She asked quickly, "John, where is your revolver?"

"In my right-hand pocket. But I, I cannot hold it." Mary reached into my pocket, drew out the revolver and cocked it. She held it firmly in both hands and aimed along the barrel at Bertrand.

"Mary, what are you doing?" It was already obvious.

Her voice trembled. "John, we have nothing more to lose."

I closed my eyes as she fired. And as the shot rang out, I prayed that she had hit the right one.

After the Fight

As I opened my eyes again, I saw one of the two stretched out on the ground, while the other stood there and then slowly approached to ensure that his opponent was really finished. The poor light and my loss of blood slowed my thoughts, and did not allow me at first to be sure whom Mary had hit. Only as the standing one threw the knife aside, and with his free hand held his injured left arm, was it clear that this was Holmes. He walked stiffly but briskly to us.

I looked back to Mary, who still held the revolver, clutching it stiffly as she stared at the man she had just shot. I spoke gently to her. "Mary, Mary my dear, it is over, you have saved us both. Come, give me the weapon now." I turned to lie back and reach up to her, with my left hand stretched out to her.

Slowly she looked away from Bertrand and to me. Her eyes were still staring, and it seemed that all colour had left her face. As if mechanically, she gave the weapon back to me, and I at once secured it. Still staring at me, she said, as I heard, in a very quiet voice, "Oh, John, John, my dearest…."

There was no more, because she broke out into a violent attack of deep, painful sobbing. With my left hand, I held her to me. With her head on my heart, she lay sobbing on my shoulder, my arm around her. I tried to reassure her, hoping my voice had some ability to convey calm and reassurance. So it was, that I felt how she slowly relaxed in my arms.

Holmes had now reached us, and I saw how pale he was. He sank on one knee beside us, and looked at us both, deeply concerned. With a tremor in his voice that I had never heard before, he said, "Thank God, Watson, that you both live. I had feared the worst, as I saw you on the ground. And when your wife fired off the shot that saved us, I felt the certainty that you were no longer alive. Never in my life was I so thankful, that I had drawn the wrong conclusion."

Despite his anxiety and his own weakness, I saw a slight smile, but it disappeared as quickly again, as he spoke. "But Watson, you are seriously injured, and you need medical care at once. We will find the police to help you. I must see where they are." He tried to stand up, but before I could speak he fell back again onto his knee, saying, "I'm so sorry, Watson, my strength fails me."

"But Holmes, do not concern yourself now; did you not hear the police whistles at the park entrance? They are not far away." And Mary at that moment lifted her head from my breast and said, with a thankful smile, "I will go to fetch them."

She thus left us for a moment, and now Holmes looked down at me again and said, in a tormented voice, "My dear Watson, I am full of remorse, that you and your wife should have been put into such terrible danger."

"But Holmes, there was no way of knowing that it might turn out like this. Let us rather think how we have avoided a much worse disaster, had the dynamite been detonated."

"That is so, but the price you and your wife might have paid was still a very terrible one."

"As I said, Holmes, it could not be foreseen, and you have also fearlessly risked your life to save Mary and me."

But Holmes insisted, "Without your wife's action, all would have been lost. We owe our lives to her courage and determination." Holmes' words had deeply moved me, and I was lost for an answer as we heard Inspector Lestrade's shrill voice, and the sound of running feet.

"My God, Mr. Holmes, Dr. Watson, I see you are indeed severely wounded, but keep calm, the police are here and will take care of everything." I saw a tired smile on Holmes' face, while Lestrade was giving his orders. We were laid gently on two stretchers, to be brought to the nearest hospital, the Dreadnought Seamen's Hospital just outside Greenwich Park. Now that the worst immediate danger was behind us, and Holmes and I were in safe hands, and Lestrade had promised to look after Mary, the relaxation became overwhelming, and I felt a wave of exhaustion threatening to submerge me. I have scarcely a recollection of the way we were taken, or how we arrived, at the hospital. I only remember that each time I opened my eyes, I found Holmes on the stretcher beside me. He seemed each time to be watching me critically, but I only wanted to sleep and become a part of the darkness that enveloped me.

In the Seamen's Hospital

A noise disturbed me and led to my awaking. As I opened my eyes, I first saw a window with bright sunshine streaming in. My gaze wandered through my surroundings. I realised, at first only vaguely, that I was in a sickroom. Was this the hospital?

I tried to remember what had happened. Gradually my memory returned, and the last thing I could recall was that Holmes and I, both wounded, had been carried here. I seemed to be reasonably well. There were heavy bandages on my right forearm and on my right thigh, which led me to think that the wounds had been well looked after and treated. But how was Holmes? What had become of him? I felt a return of my anxiety, and I was no longer calm. Where was he? I had to know. I called the nurse, but my voice would not come; my call sounded more like the grating call of a crow, and surely never reached the corridor beyond the door. I struggled to find a way to attract attention, when there was suddenly movement, and the dividing curtain in the room fluttered slightly. Thank Heaven! Someone was here, perhaps another patient, more mobile than I, who could help me. He could call the nurse. The curtain was pulled aside, and then I saw that it was Holmes himself who stood before me. I looked at him in relief, and noticed then he was pale and had his left arm in a sling. Otherwise, he seemed well on the way to recovery.

His face lit up, as he saw me and said, "Watson, my dear friend, how good it is that you are finally awake. How do you feel?" I wanted deeply to share with him my delight that he was near me, and tried to answer. The croaking voice that I heard did not seem to be mine, and I could only bring out sounds he could not begin to understand. "Dear Watson, please do not worry; I will fetch help, and the nurse will give you something to drink. Then you can speak again." I saw then that he was dressed in a hospital nightshirt and a dressing gown. He went out into the corridor.

When he returned he was accompanied by a nurse and a doctor. The two helped me and brought pillows, which enabled me, with their support, to sit up in bed. The nurse brought me a glass of water, which I drank eagerly, and the doctor described to me my condition and the treatment I had received. In my thigh, as I feared, a major blood vessel had been injured. However, thanks to Mary's prompt emergency treatment with the bandage in the park, my leg had been saved. A surgical operation had been necessary and although it had been successful, I fell afterwards into a heavy fever that lasted three days. Only last night the fever had abated, and this morning it seemed to have been overcome. When my colleague had finished his review, he asked me to move the fingers of my right hand, and the wrist, and this caused no problem. I also had no pain. Then he asked me to move my right foot and my toes. This also was successful, without pain, but when he asked me to bend my knee, there was a fierce stabbing pain in the place where the knife had entered. I told him, and he assured me that all was well, but that such a deep wound would take some time to heal. This I knew from my own experience, where the gunshot wound which I had, as a military doctor, received in Afghanistan, had also taken terribly long to heal. Then also I had fallen into a severe fever, which I might not have survived without the care of my loyal orderly. My injured shoulder could not there, in a war district, be properly treated and even now causes me pain. I hoped now that this would not be so with my right leg, and told my colleague, the hospital doctor, so. He was reassuring, indeed, optimistic, and said that as long as there were now no complications, I should be able to leave the hospital in a few days. I would, however, need a lengthy period of convalescence. My diet would have to be light, and rich in iron, so that the regeneration of blood would be enhanced. When he had explained this and glanced at my temperature record, he nodded, satisfied, and took his leave, taking the nurse with him.

"So, Watson, it seems that the prospects are good. A little time to rest and be quiet, and you will soon be your old self."

"Yes, Holmes, I think so, and perhaps the worst is now behind us. I only wish I had thought to ask the doctor to let Mary know the good news."

"Do not be concerned, dear friend, she will soon be here. She has since Saturday hardly stirred from your bedside. It was only last night, as the doctor told her that you were over the worst, that she allowed herself to be persuaded to go to Mrs. Forrester and sleep to build up her strength. She will be here at two o'clock to see if you are yet awake. Indeed, I think she is already here."

Holmes was sitting on the edge of the bed, and was looking at me, so he had his back to the door. I could not understand how he could have said such a thing. Perhaps he had only guessed, for I saw nothing. And yet – at that moment a woman entered the room, and yes, it really was my Mary. As she saw me sitting up in bed, a change came over her face, and the worried expression gave way to one of relief and happiness. She cried out, "Oh, John, John, my dearest," fell on my neck, and kissed me tenderly. Then she took my hand, held it tight and said, over and over, "Oh, John, Oh, John, I was so afraid that I might lose you…."

I saw how Holmes stood up and quietly left us in the room, alone.

After nearly an hour Holmes came back, and was quite surprised to find that Mary was no longer with me. I explained to him however that I had myself advised her that she should now go and rest, because it was obvious to me that she was suffering acutely from the lack of sleep and from the effect of her fear, He understood perfectly, and I found this a good moment to ask how he knew that she had at that moment been coming. He laughed. "Watson, I see you already feel better! But it was not difficult. If I tell you how I came to that conclusion, you will tell me that it was trivial."

"Oh, Holmes, surely not," I assured him.

"All right, then we will see:

1. Our sickroom is the last on this corridor.
2. I heard for some moments the brisk and energetic step of a young woman, and also heard the rustle of her travelling skirt.
3. These sounds were quite different from those of the nurses, which I have been hearing daily, so it had to be a visitor.
4. I knew that she would arrive at this time.

What other conclusion could I then reach, than to tell you that she was now here?"

"That was indeed simple," I replied. He looked at me with pleasure, and made no further comment.

.

There was now a pause, and I rested, but then I asked him more. "Holmes, you were talking of deduction, and that is my starting point to ask whether you can, as I hope, tell me what the Thames murders were all about. I do not feel that I have everything clear in my head."

"I would gladly do so, Watson, especially as this hospital offers little to keep a thinking mind properly occupied. But I fear that it might be too strenuous for you. Would you not rather wait until we are home again?"

"My goodness, Holmes, do you really think that having to be patient for so long, would really be conducive to my convalescence?"

Holmes smiled and sat on his own bed, in his typical cross-legged position, took the sling off his arm and closed his eyes, putting his fingertips together, to give me the following account. "Then, Watson, pay attention and I will tell you what the known facts reveal.

"Some time ago, Professor Moriarty had learnt of the forthcoming diamond auction. He determined to steal the diamonds, but a theft during the auction, or during the transport, was likely to be too risky, because of the inevitable police presence. There remained the possibility of theft from the bank safes where they were to be held, by secret government arrangement, beforehand. That introduced a new problem, of breaking in unnoticed, for a tunnel or conventional bank robbery was out of the question. He concluded that dynamite would be needed to open the safes. But he then had to obtain the required quantity of dynamite, without attracting attention.

"At this point Moriarty learned that dynamite was periodically stored by the government in the warehouse of Tucker & Son, and he saw a possibility to obtain it. There was however a problem: The only way to break into the heavily guarded warehouse seemed to be over the roof. This would allow the guards to be reached unobserved, so that they could be overpowered. Clearly the warehouse break-in must remain unobserved until the dynamite had been safely removed.

"Now Moriarty had to find out where, among his team, he might obtain the services of someone with the necessary skills – criminal, athletic and acrobatic. He had in mind both the dynamite theft, and also an attack on the theatre performance on the same evening in Greenwich Park, which he had devised as a diversion. I suspect he may only have found the answer, when something occurred in France that caught his attention. Watson, now, what do you think that might have been?" He looked at me expectantly.

I replied at once, "I think you mean the unsuccessful attempt by the Sûreté to arrest the knife thrower, Louis Bertrand."

"Just so, Watson. As I had already concluded, Bertrand must be in a most difficult situation. He was hiding from the

Sûrete and had no possibility to obtain cash, or indeed to escape from France. Professor Moriarty learned of this and ensured that Bertrand obtained new personal papers, money and a ticket to England"

"But Holmes," I broke in, fearing to interrupt his account, but caught up in a sudden thought, "Does Moriarty have then such connections also outside this country? Can he really plan criminal acts in this way?"

"Oh, yes, Watson, he is truly a Napoleon of crime. He sits like a spider in a network that reaches far outside the boundaries of Her Majesty's realms. He is aware of the least activity in these networks and, when things are threatening, or indeed useful, he can react quickly, and without scruples." As he spoke, I looked at him with increasing alarm. Although I had previously heard little of Professor Moriarty, it was becoming clear what a dangerous opponent he might be. Holmes, however, had picked up the thread of his thoughts and was continuing his narrative.

"Louis Bertrand had now an obligation to Moriarty. The first plan to be executed was that of the Thames murders. They were deliberately at first random, to conceal the real victim, away from whom attention was to be diverted. And that was…" Here Holmes made a significant pause and looked at me.

"Well, Holmes, I am sorry, but I feel there is no-one except the insurance agent from Lloyds, Mr. Williams, who might seem to fit the situation." I tried to put more conviction into my voice, to sound as assured as my friend, and began my explanation. "As I said before, Mr. Williams was probably a gambler, and would always need money for his bets. This personal weakness, together with his connections outside our country, which arose from his professional interests, were used by Moriarty to bring Louis Bertrand to England."

Satisfied that this was the correct conclusion, I looked at Holmes expectantly. Holmes looked at me with a fine smile on his lips. "Indeed, my dear Watson, as I said to you then, and can say again now, your conclusion, given the facts you have observed, appears correct." These words of praise and encouragement left me feeling somewhat satisfied, and my face showed perhaps a smile, despite the circumstances.

Holmes opened his eyes, and continued with his friendly voice, "But the facts quickly changed, and it was then clear that your conclusion must be false. Williams was another regrettable, random victim."

My smile disappeared and I could only look on with a somewhat hurt expression. "Come, now, Watson, there is no reason to be discouraged. You will soon understand why this became clear. Let us go through the evidence again, looking at all the important features. As I told you, a break-in at the bank with explosives could only be considered, if the police were somehow distracted. This distraction was to be provided by a murderous dynamite explosion in Greenwich Park, with many victims. This was where all the forces available to the police would then concentrate, and more would come, together with all possible rescue services.

"During this tragedy, which was to be played out near the bank of the Thames opposite the Isle of Dogs, Moriarty's band could count on a quiet period to conduct their attack on the strong room of the Bank of England some miles away in the City. This unprecedented and audacious robbery required that the explosion in Greenwich would take a most destructive form. It was planned that dynamite charges should be installed at critical points throughout the wooden structure of the amphitheatre and grandstand. That needed agility and acrobatic qualities, which Louis Bertrand obviously possessed. The problem was to place the charges unobserved. Can you think, Watson, how that might be done?"

He looked at me questioningly. "It would seem easiest if the person doing so were employed in the park and had full access to the site."

"Just a moment, Holmes, I remember now, Havendale, the manager of the park, told us himself that Nathaniel Cook had a friend, and that when Mr. Cook died, the friend took over the work of Nathaniel, and gave all his energy to ensure that the construction, apparently threatened by Cook's death, was completed on time. Are you then telling me that this friend of Nathan Cook was in fact Louis Bertrand?"

"Correct, Watson, and I might have thought of it earlier, if the garrulous Mr. Havendale had not distracted me."

"But Holmes, how should you have known?" I asked, rather troubled.

"Watson, I might have realised that the circus artist Louis Bertrand and Leo Baxter, the supposed friend of Mr. Cook were one and the same person. People who change identity often adopt new names with the same initials."

I had to admit that the thought of identical initials only struck me as he said it. Holmes however continued unconcerned. "The engagement in Greenwich Park would have required at least some papers. These were in the name of Leo Baxter. These were also those with which he had left France and entered England. He needed therefore no help from Mr. Williams, so with a good set of forged papers, which would assure an undisturbed crossing to England, the need for Williams' help no longer existed. Williams was, therefore, not connected with the plot."

I had followed closely, and could only add, "Indeed, Holmes, that is now clear. But were then Cook and Bertrand really friends, and was Cook also in the pay of Professor Moriarty?"

"No, Watson, and it was not even necessary. Cook was being influenced by Miss Kitty, whose promises, whatever they were, had only the aim of getting Cook to secure Bertrand's employment at the Park. With that, he would have served his purpose. Cook was however a man of honour and an upright citizen, and I think he must have become suspicious. It may even have been that he saw that Bertrand was up to mischief, a little too eager to get the job on the Theatre."

"How do you arrive at that, Holmes?"

"Well, now, Watson, just think back to the words of Miss Kitty, as she and Bertrand aired their difference at Porky's."

I struggled to remember, and it came back to me: "She said something like, *'He says he wants nothing more to do with it, and that he was going to give it all away.'* You are right, Holmes, Miss Kitty said *He* meaning Cook, and she meant that Cook was getting ready to give the game away to the police."

"Just so, Watson."

Encouraged by this, I went on, "Then Mr. Cook was the intended victim in the Thames murders series. But was he murdered because he had become suspicious?"

"Not quite, Watson, his suspicion may simply have come too soon. He was the intended victim, because he had to be killed anyway. He was, had all gone to plan, the only one who could uncover the links between Bertrand and Miss Kitty, which led back to Colonel Sebastian Moran. I do not exclude that in this, Bertrand, with Miss Kitty, had a connection to Moran, Moriarty's adjutant, whom we also heard mentioned at Porky's."

"Then Miss Kitty also had to die because she knew too much?"

"I fear so, Watson, but perhaps also because she had publicly humiliated Bertrand at the Rat and Raven. Let us not forget that he was Gallic, and very proud and quickly offended."

"Then, Holmes, there remain Mrs. Walter, the nurse; and John Miller, the dockworker, who from the start were not involved. Was it only unfortunate that Bertrand came upon them? And that he murdered them simply to create more confusion?"

"Yes, Watson, I grieve to admit that these were unscrupulous killings of innocent passers-by".

"Holmes, I believe I see now clearly, thanks to your explanations, what this was all about, and yet there is still one part which seems to be quite pointless."

"Oh, which one was that, Watson?"

"The murder of Lord and Lady Willerby. That was surely not a random killing, but a deliberate gesture then, and Bertrand proceeded quite differently. There was the story of the stolen hansom. How does it fit in?"

Holmes spoke quietly and obvious with some remorse. "Watson, I believe that I may at least in part be responsible for that crime."

"You, Holmes, surely that cannot be!" I replied, almost speechless.

"Indeed, it may be so, Watson. Do you recall that after the theft of the dynamite I spent some time incognito in the docks, to make closer enquiries?"

"I well remember, Holmes, and you admitted that you had found little of value there".

"Yes, indeed, Watson, that was so. It must, I think, have been these investigations that alerted Professor Moriarty's network to the idea that questions were being asked. I am sure he was aware of my suspicion that the Thames murders, although apparently random, were really committed, to cover for a different crime, and that I thought he was responsible. He also realised that I saw him as being behind the dynamite robbery, and he felt himself threatened as I tried to find out where the dynamite might be hidden. He knew that that question, what one person might intend to do with such a large amount of dynamite, would occupy me until I found a plausible answer.

"A political attack might have been an answer, but as I have earlier explained, this field of action was not one in which he was at all involved. As far as he could see a possibility, however, to make profit out of a political murder, he took for his next Thames murder a person out of these circles. The audience at the Charity Benefit concert at the Elephant and Castle Theatre were all politicians and their families; that gave a wide choice. It only needed that the victim, or victims, could be brought to the Thames-side district of the murders; that needed a means of transport."

"Do you mean, then, Holmes, that it could have been any member of the illustrious audience at the Charity event?

"At least, Watson, any guest who needed a hansom for the journey home, and one of them would surely do so."

For a moment we were both silent. I realised how bitter it was for Holmes that he had been deceived by Professor Moriarty's constructed scenario of a political murder. That was not primarily however because Moriarty, as if in a game, could win this point for himself, but because it had cost the lives of two good persons. Before Holmes was overcome, as could well happen, by a deeply morose mood, to fall into a long silence, I decided to ask him something directly.

"Holmes, what happened then with the planned break-in at the Bank of England? Was it prevented?"

"Yes, Watson, it was indeed. While Lestrade was with us in the Park, Inspector Gregson was on the way with a strong force to the bank. He arrived there just as the burglars were preparing to blow open the main doors. As they realised that the police were there, they fled, leaving their explosives."

I was suddenly very tired. "That was truly a pity," I was able to say, and then dropped back into my pillows. It had indeed exhausted me to listen and to concentrate while Holmes had made his explanations.

Before I slipped away into another deep sleep, I heard him say with some bitterness, "Yes, Watson, it is a great disappointment that we could not take prisoner any of the band. Now that Bertrand is dead, there is no one who can make any statement. You will see that there is not the least trace that might lead either to Colonel Moran or to Professor Moriarty. They will once more escape the law, and their just punishment. But we know, and they are aware of that. Believe me, Watson, I swear that the day will come when my hand will rest heavily on Moriarty's shoulder, and he will have to answer for his crimes, whether before an earthly judge or a higher one."

The Curtain Falls

As I awoke next morning, I was surprised to find that Holmes was already dressed and that his bag was packed. "Good morning, Holmes! What are you doing there?"

Obviously in a good mood, he looked at me cheerfully and said, "Good morning, Watson. The nurses and I were careful not to wake you. Since, however, you are now recovering, I have decided to discharge myself."

I looked at him in astonishment. However, before I could speak, he continued: "The doctors here have told me that I still need complete quiet, and would like to keep me here, in order to observe me, but this idleness is a torture for my soul. But give me the most abstruse puzzle to solve, or secret code to break, and I am in my element, and that does me good."

"Holmes, you should still take the advice of your doctors seriously. Otherwise there is a risk that you may find yourself back in hospital again sooner than you would like," I dared to say.

It seemed that my remark had somewhat reduced his almost euphoric mood, but he continued with enthusiasm, and assured me light-heartedly, "Come, Watson, don't be alarmed. Mrs. Hudson will bring all her motherly care to bear and provide for all I need. Moreover, there is no problem at present waiting to be solved, so that I can now devote myself to quite harmless amusements, such as bringing my criminal files up to date, and also find time for a chemical experiment which I had started but could not complete. In addition, there are certainly personal things to which I should attend."

In this moment I was like every other patient in hospital, envious of the fellow patient who was going home; I suddenly felt lonely and downhearted, that I would no longer have Holmes' company. I asked him, in a voice that perhaps betrayed my feelings, whether he might perhaps visit me. Holmes was ready to leave, with his travel bag packed, but he came quickly to my bedside and took my hand. "My dear friend, please forgive my selfishness. The thought of getting back to Baker Street, where, in place of weak tea and these medicines, I could now look forward to a sherry and a good pipe, has left me thinking only of myself. But don't be concerned, Watson. I spoke with your doctor, who has assured me that you should be able to leave in a week's time. I promise you, now, that when you are discharged, I will come personally to fetch you."

During this short comment I saw his troubled look change to a slight smile and his typical enthusiasm came back into his eyes. And, as so often, his frank and honest words were enough to restore me. He took my hand in both of his, pressed firmly and said cheerfully "Now, Watson, you will take good care and not overtax yourself."

"I would say the same to you," I replied, and responded with a smile. Then he turned away, took his bag and went to the door. There he paused, looked back and called, "Remember, in a week I am coming to fetch you."

I was obliged to smile, and I raised a hand to call, "Next week, Holmes." He turned, and I heard his energetic footsteps in the corridor, until they faded away, and I was again alone.

I would not bore you, dear readers, with everyday life in a hospital, even though it was clear that we had, in our emergency, enjoyed very privileged care. Let us retain the essential aspects, the principal of which was that my recovery progressed rapidly, and I felt better every day. I overcame the monotony of hospital life with extensive reading and, as soon as I was well enough, with walks in the park, accompanied by my dear Mary, who came every day to visit me. Apart from Mary I also had a visit from Mrs. Hudson, who spoiled me with a homemade cake, and from Inspector Lestrade, who wanted to thank me privately for my contribution to solving the mystery of the Thames murders.

But there then came a visitor with which I really had not reckoned, indeed would not even have considered possible: Holmes' brother Mycroft. The visit was so completely unexpected, because Mycroft Holmes moves like a planet: He has his fixed orbit, made up of the direct lines between his apartment, his Whitehall office, and the Diogenes Club. This was the man who appeared and stood in my hospital room at the Dreadnought Hospital for Seamen. That this was really so, showed me the honour he wished to pay me, and the importance which he attached to this visit. And so it proved. His purpose in visiting was to bring me thanks, in the name of Her Majesty's Government, for my part in frustrating the explosives plots, but also to remind me that the whole affair must be kept strictly confidential, until further notice, because, with the theft of the dynamite, the government of the day might be seriously compromised.

Holmes did not visit me at all in these days, and I began to fear that he had had some sort of relapse, so I asked Mary if she could find out how he was recovering. I was most surprised that Mary answered, at once, that Holmes was quite strong and full of plans. To my question, how she might know, she explained to my surprise that he had made frequent visits to her in Kensington. I was no less puzzled, when, on my asking what this was all about, she smiled to say that this was all to be a surprise for me. However much I tried, she was not to be drawn out, but assured me that all was well.

On Thursday 19th June, a week after Holmes had left the hospital, I too was allowed to leave and go home. I had dealt with the formalities and taken leave of my doctor and nurses, and was finishing packing my few possessions in my bag, when I heard a familiar and trusted voice behind me: "Good morning, Watson! "

I sprang round and saw Holmes standing there at the open door. He looked well, and was wearing a light summer suit. His face mirrored his good humour and friendly enthusiasm. "Good morning, Holmes," I said, "and be assured how pleased I am, that you are here to take me home."

We approached one another and shook hands warmly. "I see that you have packed, so, if you are ready, we can go down and take the hansom which I have waiting for you outside. So, come now, let us be on our way!" With these words he took my bag in one hand, and with the other led me out into the corridor.

As we were sitting in the cab, I thought it appropriate to ask where we were going, and so said, "Holmes, where are you taking me, to Baker Street or directly to Mary in Kensington?"

A smile spread over his face as he replied, "I will indeed bring you to your wife, but not in Kensington."

Very surprised, I looked at my friend, who looked up and laughed quietly before carrying on with his plan: "Please do not be alarmed, my dear friend; everything has been carefully and precisely planned, between myself and your wife, and is well calculated to ensure your full recovery." Curious, I waited for what came next.

"We are on the way to London Bridge station, where your good lady is awaiting you. From there you will travel to Sussex, more precisely to the country home of Mrs. Forrester, who has also gone there, while still nursing her sprained ankle. After a stay in the country, you will be soon strong enough to face again the challenges of work in your practice."

Speechless, at so much kindness, I listened to him. He was right, that such a holiday in the country would be most effective in my convalescence. The possibilities of a few relaxing days with my dear Mary, knowing that we were no burden for Mrs. Forrester, was most attractive. And yet, I could not forget that my practice would during this time remain empty, and that there would be no income during our absence. Without income I was not able to pay the costs and the repayments to the bank. That inevitably filled me with anxiety.

As if he had read my thoughts, Holmes continued: "You will surely be anxious about the practice, as is only natural. Your neighbour Dr. Smythe will however represent you, as he has assured me. The financial loss is no longer your concern; Her Majesty's Government will be responsible for this, and Mycroft has already made all arrangements. You may be reassured, that the sum involved is quite adequate not only to cover your lost income, but to pay off the remainder of the bank's loan on your practice."

I looked at Holmes, once again rendered speechless, until I could stammer, "But that is wonderful, Holmes. Yet, how does it come about, that I may expect such a reward?"

"Dear Watson, I can assure you that the past tense is already more appropriate; it has already all been resolved. I first had the repayments dealt with, and the remainder of the government's payment is now deposited at your bank. When you are back in London, we can look again at the final settlement. As for the reason, why you should be so rewarded, we only need to think of what has been achieved. We will remember that two serious attacks with explosives have been prevented, that many lives have been saved, and that the diamond robbery was also frustrated. The auction took place as planned. So will the Foreign Office's policy meeting. In addition, a most dangerous criminal, Louis Bertrand, has met his well-deserved end. You have risked your life in doing so, and endangered your health. And with the obligation to maintain silence, you cannot even recount this story in your usual way. In every way, your selfless readiness to serve others has caused you great pain and severe financial loss. That was the government's view as well."

And yet, I was uneasy. He was making it all sound too one-sided. I replied, "But, Holmes, the greater part of the work was your effort. Surely, yours should be the reward."

"Dear Watson, I have my own reward. Indeed, I have often drawn great benefit from your literary gifts in describing our adventures. What more do I need? Please allow me the satisfaction of being able to ensure the future financial well-being of my best friend."

I was embarrassed, and sank my head to reply quietly but simple, "Thank you, Holmes". Suddenly, I felt a strong pressure on my arm, obliging me to look up into his face. In a moment, his relaxed and cheerful tone had changed to a serious manner:

"Just listen now to me, Watson. You do not need to thank me, because I am the one who stands in your debt. You have made my activities famous, and always put yourself in the background. You have accompanied me in so many cases and were always loyal and faithful. I know that you would give your life to save mine. And now it is I who must thank you, for your deep and honest friendship."

Holmes' words were balsam to my heart, and moved me greatly. I was not able to speak, and so I could only take his hand and grasp it strongly. I felt how Holmes returned the pressure, and this seemed to seal the friendship we shared.

In the meantime we had reached London Bridge station, where we learned that the train for our destination in Sussex was already standing. All had been arranged, tickets were produced. Holmes had reserved for us a complete first class-compartment, so that we could enjoy the journey undisturbed. We saw that Mary was already there, walking up and down. It was a heartfelt greeting, there on the platform, before we then took our places on the train. Holmes stood there at the open door, as it was not yet time for us to leave. "I wish you both a good journey and a complete recovery. But before you leave, may I ask you a question, Mrs. Watson?"

His face was questioning, and we both nodded our agreement. "Mrs. Watson, you have had greatly to fear for your husband's safety. That is why I ask if you would prefer in the future that he no longer accompany me on my cases?"

Mary looked Holmes directly in the eyes. She weighed her words carefully as she answered, but her voice had a warm and friendly ring. "Mr. Holmes," she said, "I am the wife of a doctor, and I know that my husband takes many risks, despite all precautions. When he treats a patient with a highly infectious disease, it is always so. I pray daily that the worst may never happen; but if it did, I would be able to accept it. The profession of a doctor requires complete dedication to the sick, and John loves his profession. I for my part love John and could not wish otherwise than that he is content. I can thus accept that John may risk his life for a stranger. How could I have an objection, when I know that he stands faithfully beside his closest friend?"

Holmes followed every word, as did I; and I knew that Mary's words had stirred him too, as they did me, for there was a sudden pause. Then he asked me the next question. "And you, Watson, how is it with you? Will you come with me, when my services are again called for?"

"Whenever and wherever you wish," I said, cheerfully and glad that the tension was broken.

But time was passing, and a shrill whistle told us that our train must now depart. Holmes slammed the door, and waved a last greeting, and Mary and I waved from the open window. As long as I could I kept Holmes in view, until it really was no longer possible.

I was looking forward to our holiday and my convalescence, but I still looked forward to the day when I would again see Holmes. I had not the least idea that my wish might be granted, and under mysterious circumstances, much sooner than I thought. But that must be another story.

End

Also from Johanna M. Rieke

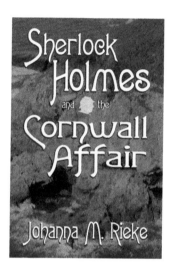

Do you love Cornwall, with its cliffs and breakers, sleepy fishing harbours and villages? Would you like to meet a real English Lord? And do you enjoy an authentic, well researched historical crime story? With the author you will accompany the renowned Baker Street detective, Sherlock Holmes, and his friend Dr Watson, on their journey to Cornwall. There, in idyllic surroundings, they are faced with seemingly impenetrable questions, leading to desperate villainy. A fifty-year-old history of intrigue, smuggling, betrayal, murder and revenge waits to be revealed, and you are there, with Holmes and Watson.

MX Publishing

MX Publishing brings the best in new Sherlock Holmes novels, biographies, graphic novels and short story collections every month. With over 400 books it's the largest catalogue of new Sherlock Holmes books in the world.

We have over one hundred and fifty Holmes authors. The majority of our authors write new Holmes fiction - in all genres from very traditional pastiches through to modern novels, fantasy, crossover, children's books and humour.

In Holmes biography we have award winning historians including Alistair Duncan, Paul R Spiring, and Brian W Pugh

MX Publishing also has one of the largest communities of Holmes fans on Facebook and Twitter under @mxpublishing.

www.mxpublishing.com

Also from MX Publishing

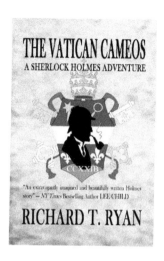

When the papal apartments are burgled in 1901, Sherlock Holmes is summoned to Rome by Pope Leo XII. After learning from the pontiff that several priceless cameos that could prove compromising to the church, and perhaps determine the future of the newly unified Italy, have been stolen, Holmes is asked to recover them. In a parallel story, Michelangelo, the toast of Rome in 1501 after the unveiling of his Pieta, is commissioned by Pope Alexander VI, the last of the Borgia pontiffs, with creating the cameos that will bedevil Holmes and the papacy four centuries later. For fans of Conan Doyle's immortal detective, the game is always afoot. However, the great detective has never encountered an adversary quite like the one with whom he crosses swords in "The Vatican Cameos.."

"An extravagantly imagined and beautifully written Holmes story"
(**Lee Child**, NY Times Bestselling author, Jack Reacher series)

Lightning Source UK Ltd.
Milton Keynes UK
UKHW020827201120
373762UK00014B/1314